Flights of Fancy

BURTON MONDAY WRITERS

DEDICATION

To Maggs Payne, founder and Honorary President of
Burton Monday Writers

Burton Monday Writers
www.burtonmondaywriters.co.uk
burtonwriters@aol.com

CONTENTS

IN MEMORY OF

Bunty Marshall (1922-2013)
A Burton Monday Writer

ACKNOWLEDGMENTS

Members of Burton Monday Writers would like to express their gratitude to a wide number of creative writing tutors who have guided, inspired and encouraged the group over the years. Special thanks to creative writing tutor Bead Roberts for her wisdom, guidance and support through the many workshops she has delivered to the group. Also, many thanks to the National Association of Writing Groups (NAWG) for their work supporting so many writing groups like Burton Monday Writers.

Burton Monday Writers would also like to thank Maria Soldano for the cover illustration inspired by the swans on the Trent beneath the Ferry Bridge and to John Carpenter for the cover artwork.

Burton Revisited by Ann Hodgkin

"What do we want to go to Manchester for?"

Lily Monsall was loud and clear with her negative comments.

I slid further into the seat. My ginger hair has faded with the years, but my tendency to blush is as lively as ever. I could feel my face burning with embarrassment as the room fell silent.

I'd never dared put forward an idea before, but Manchester seemed to me like the perfect place for the Golden Leaves outing. From Lily's derisive tone, you'd have thought I'd suggested a trip down the Amazon.

The truth is that I still feel like an outsider. I'm a bona fide Burtonian of course. I was born and bred here, but we moved to Derby when Fred got a job at Rolls Royce. After Fred died I returned to my roots, but forty years is a long time and I hardly recognise Burton now.

I thought that joining the club would help me fit in, but the group's very close knit. The members are extremely confident and they lead such interesting lives.

At the start of each meeting Muriel, our leader, asks if anyone has any news, and they're all full of fascinating snippets that they can't wait to share.

Last month Annie Bedworth's daughter was going on a round the world cruise, Bill Smythe's granddaughter-in-law had had triplets and Jennifer Morrel's son was awarded the OBE. How can I compete with all that?

"Well I think it's a brilliant idea," Bill boomed. "It's about time we went somewhere with a bit of life, and the coach journey up over the Peak will be breathtaking."

My mind lurched back to the present and I sat bolt upright again. I could hear whispers of approval from around the room. My cheeks cooled as quickly as they had reddened. Maybe Manchester was not so radical after all.

I returned to my new house feeling more at home than I had since my move. I related the tale to Minky as I served out her food.

"Miaow," she replied. Perhaps she's beginning to settle in too.

The following week was 'hobbies week'. Muriel had asked for volunteers to discuss their pastimes with the group and quite a few members had come prepared.

An elegant lady wearing a long mauve dress displayed her paintings. They were beautiful watercolours of the town's riverside. Apparently she used to be an art teacher at the High School.

Muriel showed us her tapestries. She was terribly enthusiastic and tried to persuade us all to do a few stitches on a sampler she'd prepared. I was too scared of looking a fool to give it a try.

Bill Smythe brought a bunch of fabulous tea roses from his garden. He raffled them off for club funds and I won. They look lovely in my cut-glass bowl, standing on the front room window sill.

"Maybe I should have taken my beer mat collection," I said to Minky.

She arched her back, turned away and wandered slowly into the kitchen. I guess she's right. I can't see them being impressed to know that I was brought up in a public house.

The day came for the trip to Manchester and I felt very apprehensive. What if it was a disaster? It would be my fault.

It was a lovely coach. It had seat belts, air conditioning, and little pleated curtains at the windows. There was even a drinks machine so that we could have tea or coffee on the journey.

Most of the members sat with their cronies and I was left on my own. I don't mind being Jilly no-mates, but it does rather set you apart when you're on the edge of a group. Then, to my surprise Bill Smythe came to sit beside me. I told him how much I enjoyed his roses. He promised to bring me some more before the end of the summer.

He was right about the scenery. The views above Buxton were spectacular, and Bill's very knowledgeable. He pointed out the landmarks and told lots of anecdotes about the Peak villages.

Muriel had catered for our individual tastes.

We could choose whether to be dropped off at Salford Keys, or to go on to the city centre.

When I said I fancied the Keys because I'd read about it in *Woman's Weekly*, Bill decided to visit there too. So did Muriel and the lady in the mauve dress, (although she was wearing sage green on this occasion). Lily Monsall said she wanted to shop at Harvey Nicks, and to take a look at Piccadilly Gardens, so the others all opted for the city centre too.

The four of us made for the art gallery. I've always loved looking at pictures. Fred took me to the National Gallery once.

I recognised the photograph in the entrance, and then I saw the picture I'd been looking for. I didn't say anything to the others. I didn't want to appear boastful, but I felt very excited. Iris – she of the mauve dress – was in full flow telling us about the paintings and it would have seemed rude to interrupt her.

On the journey home I told Bill about my beer mats and - what a coincidence? We discovered that all those years ago when I was a barmaid in my parents' pub, Bill was working at the beer mat company across town. I've probably got the very mats that Bill printed. He promised to come round the next day to have a look.

Muriel and Lily led a sing song, but I'm not one for community singing. Bill says he's got a voice like a ship's siren in distress, so we just sat back and listened to the commotion.

When I got home I told Minky we were going to have our first visitor, but she was in a bit of a huff. She doesn't like being left on her own all day, especially as I'd locked the cat flap. I worry she'd get lost if she went out on her own.

True to his word Bill arrived at my door the following day. He was carrying the biggest bunch of roses I had ever seen.

He was fascinated by my collection and he remembered the Blue Posts. He used to drink there as a young man in the 60's, so I may well have I pulled him a pint.

I told him, in confidence of course, about the picture I'd spotted in Manchester.

"I'm there right at the front," I told him, "in my pink skirt and black jumper, shouting 'Hello' to Mrs. Waters and her baby Harry. I'd know that pram anywhere."

Then I fetched out my special beer mats. The ones I keep wrapped up in tissue paper at the back of the sideboard.

"Well I never," said Bill, as he studied the sketches on the back of the mats. "There's no mistaking who drew these."

"I can't wait to tell the Golden Leaves club about them," I confessed. "I didn't want to mention them until I was sure. By the way, how's your granddaughter-in-law and the triplets?"

I thought he was having a seizure. He covered his face with his hands and coughed and spluttered so much that I became quite alarmed, until I realised he was laughing.

"It's my time for confessions now," he roared. "I haven't got a granddaughter-in-law, in fact I haven't even got a grandson. I made it up to impress that snobby clique."

I joined in the laughter and Minky came to see

what all the noise was about.

She quite took to Bill. She leapt up onto his knee and went to sleep. He couldn't bear to disturb her, so he had to stay for a second cup of tea.

You should have seen Muriel's face when I told them at news time. Lily Monsall looked beside herself with envy.

But Iris was lovely. She's a Lowry fan, and was fascinated by the drawings on the beer mats. She agreed that they matched exactly the people in the painting of the level-crossing, she even recognised the one of me.

I'd no idea who he was when he came to the pub with his pal, but I guessed he was special. And when I read in the Mail that Mr. Lowry used to come to Burton on holiday I worked out the connection.

Bill is going to take me to Salford Keys again soon, so that I can show my pictures to the curator.

As I walked through the front door, Minky came to greet me. I've never heard her purr so loudly. Just wait until I tell her that Bill's coming to tea tomorrow and we're going to have salmon to celebrate.

The Fat Pound by Lynda Turner

Footsteps pound after me. I try to run. My legs don't work. A strong hand grabs my shoulder, the other twists my arm painfully up my back. It's a man, a uniformed officer. He slaps restraints around my wrists. They hurt. His lips always curl into a wry smile when he steps around to face me. Always the same face, in my dreams, never in life.

"I've done nothing wrong!" But my protests are in vain.

"If I'd a quid for every time I've heard that, I'd be a rich bloke, instead of pounding the beat banging up slobs."

My nostrils twitch as his foul breath nears my face. I don't want to breathe but know I must. "Honestly, I've done nothing," I plead, knowing my words are falling on deaf ears.

"Then why were you trying to leg it?"

"I was…" My body stiffens, my throat dries, words won't form but I know what's coming. He scans me with his handheld body monitor and it bleeps back the information, making the same calculations it always does.

"Central Control says you're 50 pounds above legal weight for your height and age. I'm arresting you for gross obesity. Anything you say will be recorded and read out at your hearing and failure to comply with the state law will result in further punishment. Understood?"

"Er…" No words. No defence. Nothing. I wriggle, squirm, struggle but the automatic stinger attached to the hand restraints zaps me and I go limp.

His powerful hand grabs my upper arm and hauls me up. "Use your head love, this isn't the first time you've been pulled in. You know the form."

I take his advice and come quietly. He keys my code into central terminal notifying the Fat Pound that they've got another inmate tonight. He escorts me to the fat van and deposits me inside. I'm the only occupant, there's plenty of room for more but there's never anyone else.

Soon we're moving along the highway, at least, it feels like a road, but I can't see out. I'm trapped. My hands are still cuffed, but this time in front of me. I look down at them. Familiar, they are always my hands. How did they get from behind my back to my lap? Did he remove the restraints? I can't remember. It's not important. I know we are close to the Fat Pound. It won't be long.

"All right in there?" he asks over the intercom. I make no reply. I know the form. He repeats the question. I do nothing. He stops the engine. I sink to the floor. I play dead. He yanks open the door. "And you can stop playing stupid games," he snarls, "or would you like me to add wasting police time to your charge sheet?"

I take no notice. It makes no difference. The outcome is always the same.

I hear the click as he arms his stun gun. I know what he is going to do. He climbs into the vehicle. He prods me with his foot. I feel it around my left calf but still I don't budge. He shouts, "Get up or I'll fire."

His warning goes unheeded, it has to be. I have to convince him that the round podgy figure lying on the floor of the van can't possibly hurt him. I wait for the sound of his knees clicking as he squats alongside me. He should have learnt by now to restrain my feet. I spring to life, kicking the gun from his hand, then a double kick blow to his ribs. He's winded and staggers backwards, striking his head on the bench.

No time to think. No time to plan. I've done this before. I know the form. I take control, seize his monitor, punch a few buttons, tell it to ERASE my code and details. The stun gun lies abandoned. I grab it and aim at the officer letting him have a full dose. "That'll teach you," I cry triumphantly, "if you think you're taking me to the Fat Pound you've another think coming." Jumping down from the van, I don't look back, I don't care about the officer. I'm free.

I wander around the streets. Streets I don't know, I'm lost. I'm alone but I don't feel scared. There's nobody about, nobody to harm me, nobody to see me. I come to a row of shops, all closed. Pass windows of stick models wearing straight skimpy dresses, short skirts, long thin legs, impossibly narrow jeans. The models stare back at me. I expect them to move and I wait. Nothing happens.

The next store is a gym. Suddenly it's full of people. I go inside. I'm wearing a track suit, it must be enormous, it's far too big for me.

A six pack Adonis greets me with a broad tooth-whitened smile, "We're ready now for your work out."

My mouth drops open, I've not been here before, this shouldn't happen. I'm supposed to wake up once I get out of the Fat Patrol officer's clutches. But this guy is new, he's physically toned, he's gorgeous. Why is such a beautiful man bothering to talk to me? I let him lead me to the exercise machines. I go willingly.

"We've worked out a programme for you," he flashes me a smile. I'm taken in, speechless I ogle him, I'd agree to anything. "I'll just set the machine going." He fiddles with the touch screen panel. "Just gentle exercise to start."

I want to reach out to him, touch his smooth glistening skin, run my fingers along his taut muscles, wrap my legs around...

I'm walking, slow pace at first. My legs are moving. Joy. They never work when I confront the officer. Here in the gym, things are different, I feel welcome. The pace quickens and my whole body starts to wobble. Faster. It's taking me all my concentration to keep up, to stay on the treadmill. Anxiety bites, I gasp for air, I can't keep up. I reach for the off switch. Nothing happens.

Where's the Adonis now? Gone, along with everyone else. I'm alone, attached to an out-of-control treadmill. I can't stop it. It's getting faster and faster. Blood pressure soaring, body heat climbing, it takes all I've got to fight the exercise machine. I scream aloud and wake myself up.

Exhausted, I lean back onto soft pillows, slowly letting my body rest, until I've regained control. Inwardly I curse myself for being taken in by handsome broad shoulders, tapered waist and narrow masculine hips. Where is he now? Gone.

I struggle downstairs to the kitchen, open the fridge and bathe in the cooling air. Then I see it, a huge chocolate cake, covered with whipped cream and cherries. I want a piece so much, I want to reach out and dip my finger into the soft, cool swirls of cream. But I daren't. I know the dream. I know the form. I've heard about the Fat Pound. I satisfy my cravings with a glass of milk and sit at the kitchen table wondering how many more times must I dream the dream.

Yesterday's newspaper is lying idly on the table, a tabloid. *Fat Pounds for UK* screams the headline. It's all coming true. My nightmare, but will I escape the officer when he arrests me for real? I shudder at the thought.

Reluctantly I return to bed. I'm very tired but part of me doesn't want to sleep, doesn't want to get arrested again, doesn't want to go to the Fat Pound. I've never been there, not yet, even in my dreams, I've never been through the doors. They don't exist, not yet. But I drift off to sleep, I must have because it's light when I wake, another day, a new start.

I take out my eating plan, I weigh out my breakfast. I make up my packed lunch, all within the permitted allowances. In the bathroom, I ignore the scales, I daren't get on. I clip my pace counter onto my belt. I set off for the bus stop, no, not the nearest one.

At the office I take the stairs, greet my colleagues before wiring myself up to my terminal. I've several calls waiting, I deal with them quickly. Call centre work is quick-fire, no time to break, no time to waste, no time to think about the next meal. I smile at the clients I never see, I tap their details into my computer and update their records. I'm glad I'm busy, no time to think about the dreams.

Lunch outside, it's warm. I walk, noting how many steps I've managed to clock up on my counter. I'm on target, I should make ten thousand by the end of the day. On the way back to the office, I think about the Adonis. I'd like to meet him again, but there's no way I'm going on one of his machines.

It's Wednesday, Slimming Club after work. I turn up at the library meeting room, it's busy, there's a queue. Must be the new legislation, people don't want to be fined or sent to the new Fat Pounds, when they're opened. I wait patiently for my turn, chat to the woman in front, pick up a magazine. It's full of slimming success stories. I want to be one of them, I want to stop the nightmares.

"Hello," says the consultant cheerfully, "have you had a good week?"

"Not too bad," I answer. I never tell her about the nightmares. I strip off as much clothing as is decent, including my shoes, and step onto her scales. We have to wait for the bleep, the same bleep as the officer's body monitor.

"You've lost three pounds," she tells me, "well done, only a few more pounds to your target."

For the first time today I feel really happy, I'm only a few weeks away from my ideal weight. Ideal for me because I know once I'm there, the nightmares will stop. The Adonis? I'll keep looking for him.

A Moveable Feast by Ann Hodgkin

The bang lingered in Alice's ears. The windows rattled and the saucepans jangled. Her hands were shaking and she could feel her bottom lip starting to tremble.

****

Ten minutes earlier in the quiet solitude of the house next door, Jovita had sunk slowly onto her knees. In spite of the carefully placed pillow, her joints creaked as she settled her weight. On weekdays she'd taken to saying her prayers sitting on the edge of her bed, but today was The Lord's Day and she felt it only proper to kneel.

She took her rosary from the shelf and prayed in her mother tongue. Since Stefan's death, her command of English had almost deserted her. She paused as she reached the end of her devotions.

What was that bang?

Anya, her visitor from the Polish centre, had

told her that a young woman with a child had moved into number eleven.

Jovita listened again. Through the thin walls of the terraced house she could hear the sound of loud uncontrollable gasps of misery.

She stood in the doorway and glanced along the street before hesitantly stepping outside. "Agoraphobic" Anya called it when she'd stopped venturing out, but this was different. She had to be strong. She needed to go to the aid of a neighbour in distress.

She climbed down the step, ignored the pain from her stiff knees, and knocked firmly on the adjacent door.

****

"Can we play a game now?" Benjy asked in a pleading tone, as he appeared in the doorway of the kitchen.

"In a minute sweetheart, Mummy needs to fix the cooker first," replied Alice with doubtful optimism, as she hugged Benjy to her.

A smoky patch surrounded the plug, and to Alice's inexperienced eye it seemed that the bang was terminal.

"I wanted this to be perfect," she sobbed, "our first dinner in our new home, and now I can't even cook the chicken."

Benjy clung to his mother and started to cry in sympathy, his game forgotten.

The knock on the door made them both jump.

"What now?" Alice wailed.

She opened the door cautiously, unwilling to reveal her plight to a casual caller.

"Yes, what do you want?" she barked, regretting her tone, even as she spoke.

Jovita almost retreated at the rebuff, but a glimpse at the mother's distressed face made her stand firm.

"I am Jovita," she said gently. "I come to help."

To Jovita's dismay, her offer triggered more tears. Between sobs Alice explained her plight. Jovita threw her arms around mother and son and took control.

"We'll put your chicken in MY oven," she declared. "We will prepare vegetables and eat together in my home."

To Jovita's delight Benjy laughed and squealed excitedly.

"How will I ever repay you?" Alice gasped.

"You are welcome, I will enjoy." Jovita beamed.

Alice and Benjy escorted Jovita back to her home, carefully carrying the food for the meal.

"We must go back and get ready," said Alice, patting her dishevelled hair self-consciously.

"I will wait for you around noon," agreed Jovita.

As she lit her oven and placed Alice's chicken inside, she remembered how empty her cupboards were.

Anya kindly shopped for her everyday needs, but she would like something more to offer to her young neighbours. Alice had provided the chicken and vegetables. She didn't want to appear inhospitable.

Then she thought of the corner shop. She'd

already ventured out to her neighbours' house, it wouldn't take much more courage to walk to the grocery store.

****

Sitara fidgeted on her high stool. The silk of her sari slid against the plastic seat, making it impossible to sit in comfort. Baby Asha slept peacefully in the carrycot, perched on the sacks of potatoes, but three year old Kadeem poked and prodded everything within his reach as he squirmed between the packages on the floor.

Trust Ravi to insist on opening today, she thought. He knew how she hated working in the shop, she'd got enough to do looking after the children. He'd gone to their other business on the far side of the town. Cheryl, the manager, flatly refused to work on Sundays. It was too bad of him to give in to Cheryl. Didn't he care about the needs of his own wife?

"We had a break at Diwali," he'd reminded her, when she'd protested.

The sound of the shop door opening startled Sitara. She hurried forward to steady the elderly customer, who stumbled breathlessly into the shop. Kareem gazed up at the old lady, and gave her his most dazzling smile.

Jovita reached out her hand and Kareem gripped it in his chubby fist. Sitara smiled as she saw the instant rapport between the old lady and the trusting toddler.

"You have oranges, bananas, apples?" enquired the newcomer. "And bread, milk and lemonade, thank you?"

Sitara produced a box from beneath the

17

counter, and carefully filled it with the things Jovita needed. Kareem watched, beaming happily.

"Number nine is my home," announced Jovita, as she paid the bill. "I'm pleased to meet your lovely children. I do not shop often, but I have guests today. You wish to come too, please?"

Sitara warmed to this charming lady with her friendly face and her funny accent.

"I would love to come," she replied. "I will close the shop at noon and deliver your shopping to your door. We would love to join you."

Never mind what Ravi said. She deserved a break and making new friends was just what she needed.

****

As soon as they crossed Jovita's threshold, Alice and Benjy felt at home. Benjy settled on the hearthrug with his toys, while his mother and Jovita set the vegetables to cook.

"The lady from the shop, and her children, will join us soon." explained Jovita, as she and Alice laid the table.

****

Giorgio stood in his doorway at number fourteen. For the first time in his life he was bored, bored and lonely.

"Oh how I miss you," he muttered.

He thought of Giorgio junior and his family. They'd escaped the cold, grey English weather. Their Mediterranean blood had made the lure of Oz irresistible. If he'd been a little younger he'd have joined them.

He looked forward to their letters and their sunny snapshots, but they were no substitute for his loved ones' company. Today would have been a good day for business. The first weekend of spring always brought the customers flocking, but the chimes ringing in his ears were only memories.

He caught sight of Sitara struggling along the street with the baby under her arm. She was pushing a buggy loaded with a large box, and if he wasn't mistaken, next to the box was perched a large cooking pot. Her little boy skipped behind clinging to her flowing sari.

"Let me help you!" he shouted, pleased to find someone to chat to.

He hurried across the road, and took the handle of the buggy.

****

As soon as she heard the knock Jovita hurried to the door, her sore knees forgotten in the excitement.

She recognised Giorgio at once. He and Stefan had been good friends. Many years ago they'd bonded in the local pub.

"Come and join our party," she greeted him, as Sitara and the children stepped inside.

"Please stay," added Sitara. "I have bought some lamb korma to add to the feast, there is plenty for everyone."

****

Ravi hadn't seen a soul for over an hour. He wondered how Sitara was doing. She was right, he should have listened to her. The shops traded steadily on weekdays, in fact they provided a good income, but Sundays were always slack.

He frowned as he thought of Sitara. She'd seemed so sad and anxious since Asha's birth. He knew how hard it was trying to adapt to this strange country, especially with two children to care for.

"I'll go back early and surprise her," he said to himself.

He parked his car outside his home and pushed the shop door. He was looking forward to seeing his wife's surprised face. But the door didn't yield. He pushed harder but still it didn't open.

Where was his wife? Was she ill? Had one of the children had an accident? If only he'd remembered his key.

He hurried down the deserted street, hoping to find someone who knew where Sitara had gone.

The door of number nine was ajar. He tapped sharply on the window, but there was no response.

He could hear the sound of voices and of children's laughter. The aroma of food reached his nostrils. It must be a party. Warily he entered the house.

To his surprise, the first person he saw was Sitara and she was smiling. It was so long since he'd seen her smile that he'd forgotten how beautiful she was. His children were there too. They were safe. None of the dreadful things he'd imagined had happened.

The table was laden with steaming food and everyone was tucking in.

Sitara was the first to notice him standing in the doorway. "This is Ravi, my husband," she said proudly.

"Welcome to my home," Jovita greeted him, shaking his hand. "Help yourself to the food," she invited, as she passed him a plate.

A relieved Ravi willingly joined in the fun.

Later that afternoon, Jovita reviewed the events of the day. She hadn't enjoyed herself so much for a long time, certainly not since Stefan's death.

The meal had been amazing. The roast chicken, lamb korma and vegetables may have been an unconventional mix, but everyone enjoyed it. Afterwards Giorgio had fetched a large tub of his mouth-watering Italian ice cream for them all to share, and with the fruit it had proved a delicious finale to the feast.

From the kitchen Jovita could hear Alice and Sitara chatting happily as they washed the dishes. Baby Asha was sleeping peacefully in her buggy, while a relaxed Ravi crawled on all fours with Kadeem and Benjy riding on his back.

Jovita smiled at Giorgio dozing in an easy chair in front of the television, waiting for 'Songs of Praise' to begin. Her face glowed with contentment as she felt the warmth of the friendships blossoming all around her. She would never forget this special day.

Tomorrow in her prayers she would give thanks for Alice's explosion, and silently pray that the cooker would not be fixed for a very long time.

New Beginnings by Carol Bennion-Pedley

Snow. She looked up in wonder at the beautiful flakes of snow and closed her eyes in order to feel those flakes melting upon her face. She gasped. They felt like silk across her skin, not ice. She became aware of people around her, one either side of her holding an arm each. And as she looked down, she was surprised to see that the snow just wasn't melting at all. As she put her foot forward she tried to tread on a flake and she laughed out loud when it attached itself to her shoe instead. It was pure magic and it was all for her. She carried on laughing out loud, even as the people leading the way moved her to a sparse room, undressed her and put her to bed.

The following day, she had forgotten all about the 'snow' and the magic and was only really aware of the headache she had. She knew from experience that the headache only got worse when she opened her eyes so, for now, she kept them closed. It was when she began to feel slightly sick that she knew the time of day had come again when she needed her next fix. She lifted her arm to put her hand over her eyes to shield herself from the light coming through the window. Strange, she knew what the light did to her nowadays, the curtain was never opened. What was the curtain doing open today?

It was only a brief thought, quickly overridden by the question of whether there was any more gear left in the house or would she have to go buy some more.

She put her hand to her mouth and felt the dryness there, along with a couple of cold sores she had. She had to get up. Perhaps a cigarette would help? Without opening her eyes, she put her hand out toward the general area of the bedside table she had and patted the top of it trying to find the crumpled box and the lighter beside it. Her hand knocked a bottle over but she carried on patting the table and frowned as it appeared to be virtually empty of anything at all. She usually put her hand in some kind of rubbish or tissue before she found the cigarettes.

She had to risk it. Turn over and open her eyes and see what was going on. The pain shot through her head as she did just that. The bedside table was old but clean; a few scratches on it but the only item the knocked over water bottle. Her heart started to beat just that little bit harder and she felt her skin flush and her pores broke into a cold sweat. She opened her eyes wider and the pain shot through her head again. She began to shiver and she realised she was in her underwear.

She sat up and pulled the quilt around her

shoulders. She noticed her clothes and shoes neatly stacked in the corner. There was a window opposite the bed, covered in bars. She wasn't at home. Prison then? She got up and walked to the window, her hand automatically moving to her forehead to shield her eyes again.

There was a large tree outside, mostly green leaves covering it now but there was a coating of blossom, going brown, covering the grass underneath. There was blossom on the carpet beneath her feet; that must be where it had come from. She felt the queasiness rise in her again and turned to the sink in the corner of the room. She just made it before she dry heaved into it. She had nothing in her stomach to bring up this morning, not even the water she craved. Still, this was a regular occurrence so her stomach didn't cramp up as much as it used to.

The pain in her head was getting worse now and she felt the stirrings of panic. She really, really needed a cigarette at the very least. She walked slowly to the door, not knowing where she was or what to expect. She pushed down on the door handle. It was locked. There was a peephole in the door but when she looked through she realised it was for people looking in at her, not for her benefit.

She got scared and banged her fist on the door a few times. She shouted, "Hello? Is anyone out there? Let me out!" She put her ear to the door but couldn't hear anything.

She took a step back and kicked the door with the flat of her foot a couple of times. She heard the key being put in the lock and a deep voice shouted for her to go and sit on the bed. She did as she was told and looked toward the door as it opened. A large gentleman pushed on the door and stood aside to let someone else in. A middle aged woman dressed casually in jeans and a t-shirt entered the room, followed by the large man and a woman, both dressed in white trousers and jacket; some kind of uniform.

She felt the first stirrings of real fear about what was happening. Prison wouldn't be ideal but at least she could smoke and get her drugs in there. The casually dressed woman was talking to her and she tried to focus. Something about recovery, reaching rock bottom and her sister was mentioned too. A vague memory came into focus. She had phoned her sister, hadn't she? She couldn't quite recall. She put her head in her hands and moaned. The woman was still talking but she couldn't possibly concentrate on the woman's words right now so she put one of her hands up to stop her.

"Can I at least have some aspirin?" she said quietly.

The male nurse walked over and put two pills in her hand and passed her the bottled water. She put them in her mouth and swallowed half the water immediately.

"I want to stop," she said. "Do what you have to do."

A week later, all she wanted to do was die and deep down she knew why the room was so sparse and there were bars on the window. There was nothing in the room that she could use to hurt herself with. Well, not hurt herself, she was already hurting. Kill herself, that's what she would have done if she could.

There was a basic steel toilet in the corner of the room, out of the eye-line of the peephole, not that she particularly cared at the moment about who saw her.

She divided her time between sitting on the toilet with the seemingly constant diarrhoea she had and lying in the bed.

Her skin looked like a piece of cloth pulled taught over her skeleton, as she shivered and cried out with the pain.

There was the odd moment of clarity and she spent those few precious moments looking out the window at 'her' tree, as she thought of it. It was now fully green, there was no blossom left on it at all and sometimes there was a breeze and it looked like the tree was waving encouragement at her.

At the end of two weeks in that place, she no longer thought she needed to worry about a way to die, her body was doing it for her. Her face and shoulders had broken out in spots, there were more cold sores around her mouth, her muscles constantly felt like they were burning from the inside and the headaches – she thought she would go mad from the headaches. It wasn't even as though she could escape through sleep. Her arms and legs twitched and ached all the time and sleep was almost impossible.

****

Three months later, she lay on her bed one morning, her hands behind her head and looked out of the window at 'her' tree. There was a slight breeze outside and she watched as some of the leaves that had turned brown blew from the tree, leaving a branch or two bare. She allowed herself a small smile as the realisation hit that her flu-like symptoms had entirely gone now.

The last few weeks she had been assigned an experienced member of the work team to shadow her;

someone who had gone through the same thing themselves, once. It had helped, having someone to talk to, someone who understood. As had the group therapy – she didn't feel so alone.

And tomorrow she was having her first visit, her sister, her saviour really.

****

Christmas time. She awoke to see her tree through the window, completely bare now, stripped back to its core, ready to start again. She felt like that herself, completely stripped back to her bare soul. She got up, washed and dressed, herself now the experienced member of the team, assigned to look after someone newly admitted.

She was shocked to meet the newbie. Had she truly once looked like that? She held her as she had once been held. She listened to her and understood.

****

The beginning of spring came. She sat on the bed, hands in her lap and her small suitcase by her side. The door opened and her sister stood in the doorway.

"Are you ready?" asked her sister.

Ready? For the outside world again? It was what she wanted more than anything. And yet here she was safe. It was easy here. She stood up anyway and picked up her bag.

"I am," she replied.

As she walked through the door, there was a slight breeze and a couple of pink blossom drifted in front of her. She looked over and there stood her tree. Beautiful and full of life. She smiled and carried on walking.

Winged Victory by Shelagh Wain

Pat Sanderson had enjoyed the weekend with her daughter's family. She was still smiling at the memories when she turned into Marsh Crescent and saw a tramp huddled in the bus shelter. He didn't smile back.

Her smile faded as she drove round the bend and saw her garden. The path was no longer lined with tulips and daffodils. A few fragments lay on the remains of the tiny lawn, which was covered in bare patches and spotted by smelly brown heaps.

As she climbed out of her Yaris a large man emerged from the house next door, scratching his paunch under a black T-shirt printed with the words: *Don't even think about it.*

"Afternoon, Pat. You left your gate open when you left. My dogs got in. They could've been poisoned with some of them weird plants. Should be more careful — you don't want me claiming compensation."

"You know perfectly well I latched the gate. I always do. Those dogs have been in here every day while I was away."

The paunch advanced towards her. An unshaven face loomed over her, breathing out the smell of stale beer.

"You calling me a liar? I don't like that. My lass is bringing the grandkids round on Saturday. You'd better watch it."

Pat felt her heart beating too fast as she was forced to back away. But Dave Knowles had had his fun for the day and went back into his house. Pat unloaded her luggage and put the kettle on. As she took her cup of tea into her sitting room, the music began – thumping through the party wall, driving her back into the kitchen. She burst into tears.

It wasn't fair. She and Ted had been happy in Marsh Crescent for 40 years, and she didn't want to leave now. Even if the council would re-house her, they wouldn't give her a place with a garden. Ted would have sorted out that awful man. She was sure he was a coward underneath. But Ted had been gone two years, taken from her by a heart attack a year before Dave Knowles moved in next door.

Pat tried to keep busy, sorting her clothes for the washing-machine and putting away the food she had bought on her way home. But Dave's heavy metal bands had given her a headache, and the thought of eating made her feel sick. She took her library book to bed and managed to ignore the music.

The week got steadily worse. When she got down on her knees to clean the mess from her lawn Dave leaned over the fence and shouted "Lardarse!" The music thumped away every night, and most of the day too. The only respite was to go out early in the day, before Dave got up.

On the Wednesday she saw that the curtains were still drawn and walked fast along the Crescent towards the shops at the end, almost colliding with the tramp, who was heading for his shelter. The stench made Pat step back into the road. He made as if to catch her, but thought better of it and huddled down in his filthy duvet.

Ten minutes later, Pat was sitting in her friend Marjorie's kitchen, pouring her heart out.

"Why don't you tell the Council?" Marjorie asked.

"It's not that easy. Dave isn't just a mindless thug – he's cunning. I did speak to the Council, and they sent someone round. But Dave had the music off before she got out of her car When she went to speak to him he was all friendly concern. Said he'd tried to help me, but I wouldn't talk to him. By the time he'd finished the social worker had me down as some terrible old snob who was probably losing her marbles. She was quite sharp with me. And to cap it all we've got a tramp who's taken up residence in the bus shelter. I nearly fell in the road today trying to dodge the smell!"

They both laughed. Just talking to her friend had made Pat feel better. Her good mood continued while she did a bit of shopping in the parade on the main road. It couldn't last. As she left the newsagent's she saw Dave coming towards her, his two dogs in tow.

He followed her closely as she set off home, the dogs snarling and snapping at her heels. They were some kind of bull terrier cross; even on a lead they terrified her.

The bigger dog bared its teeth and jumped up at her just as she reached the bus shelter. She was so frightened she felt faint, and had to sit down on the seat– right next to the tramp, who smelled as bad as ever.

Dave stopped, leering triumphantly as the smaller dog lifted its leg against the edge of the shelter. "Can't even manage to walk home from the shops? They'll be putting you in a home next, and I can get my lass in your house!"

Pat had to fight back the tears as she realized what he was planning. She couldn't let him win; she staggered to her feet, but fell back against the tramp. This time he did put out an arm to save her. When she set off to walk again he stood up and blocked Dave's path.

"Get out of my way, you useless lump of shit!" said Dave.

The tramp said nothing. He set off behind Pat so that the dogs could not bother her, ignoring Dave's insults. Pat plodded on without looking back, and only realized that she was free of both of them when she could no longer smell either dogs or man.

The next morning she saw Dave leave his house. Signing-on day. He would be gone for over an hour. She thought about using the time to work in her garden, but changed her mind. She walked along to the bus shelter. The tramp was huddled in his duvet, his face blue with cold. She stood quietly on the opposite side of the street and studied him. He was younger than she had thought, and not so threatening.

Years of nursing had taught Pat to trust her

instincts about people. She crossed the road. "You were kind to me yesterday. Would you like to come and have a cup of tea?"

He stayed silent for what seemed like hours. "You got anything stronger?" His voice was hoarse.

"No", said Pat firmly. "But I've got a nice warm fire."

Very slowly, he got to his feet, folded up his filthy duvet and stuffed it into a black bin bag, which he hoisted over his shoulder, then looked at her expectantly. They set off down the street.

When she had settled him into an old chair in her kitchen diner, Pat made a pot of tea. She added a small dose of 'medicinal brandy' to one mug.

"Well," she said brightly, "we've both been in the wars haven't we!" When she saw the tramp's face she could have bitten off her tongue. "I'm sorry. You're a soldier, aren't you?"

"Was." There was a long pause. "I'll be off now."

"You haven't finished your tea!"

"I wanted tea. Not pity."

"I'm not offering pity! I need your help. Please sit down and let me explain." Pat reached for his hand and saw that he had a nasty, festering cut, but she said nothing. The tramp sat down again and listened carefully while she told him everything Dave Knowles had done, ending with the threat about 'the lass'.

"Would you come and see me again at the weekend?" she asked. "I'd feel safer, knowing you were there."

"I'll think about it. Thanks for the tea."

Pat wanted to clean and dress the wound on

his hand, but she let him go. One step at a time.

On Friday Pat had a brief respite; Dave had spent the previous evening out with his mates and was now sleeping it off.

On Saturday morning, 'the lass' dropped off her two sons before going out with her friends. Pat dreaded these occasions. The boys were even less civilized than their grandfather, who left them to run wild in the garden. At lunchtime, she could hear shrieks of laughter and noticed bits of dirt in her garden. The two boys were on top of the Dave's shed, tearing pieces off the roofing felt and throwing them over the fence. She went out into her garden and approached - not too near. "You shouldn't be doing that – it will damage the roof and…"

"Who cares what you think, you fat slag," shouted the eldest boy.

"We're going to tell Grandad on you!" said the other.

Sure enough, ten minutes later there was a hammering at her front door. "Come out here, you old bitch, before I come in and get you!" One of Dave's dogs was leaving its trademark on her lawn.

Pat kept the door locked these days, so she opened her front room window. "Go away!"

"You go near my grandkids again – you so much as look at them, and I'll have you locked up. Do you understand?" He went up to the window, which Pat hastily closed.

"I was only trying to save your-"

"Save! What could you save? You're a pervert who shouldn't be let near children!" He thumped the window so hard it shook in the frame.

"Leave her alone!" The tramp was standing by

the gate.

"You again! Mind your own business, before I make you."

"The younger man said nothing, but rolled up his sleeves and moved very close to Dave. There was a tattoo on his right forearm. When Dave saw it he went pale and backed off.

"I've said me piece. She knows she'd better behave." He retreated to his own territory.

"Please come inside, Mr…"

"Watts. Kieran Watts."

Once they were inside Pat came to a decision. "I'll put the kettle on now, but I wondered if…you'd like to have a bath?" The words came out in a rush.

Kieran actually smiled. "OK," he said.

Pat put a clean towel in the bathroom and an old shirt of Ted's. When Kieran emerged he looked a good deal more human. He drank his tea, and let Pat dress the cut on his hand. She didn't ask how he got it.

Then he left the house and she didn't see him again; the bus shelter was empty.

That evening there was no music thumping through the walls. Instead, Pat heard the shrieks of 'the lass': "Live next door! You must be joking. Just because me Mam skivvied for you all her life you needn't think I'll do the same."

Pat allowed herself a smile.

It was a week before Dave started up his persecution again. He was following her with the dogs one day when a young man crossed the street to join her.

"Hello," he said.

She had to look twice. "Kieran?"

Then he turned round and looked coolly at Dave Knowles. The larger dog snarled at him but he stared it down. "You shouldn't let them jump up at people like that. They need training."

"I'll do what I like…" Dave shut up when he saw the tattoo again, pulled the dogs back and hurried on his way.

As they watched Dave and his dogs retreat, Kieran told Pat that he'd made contact with a charity which would help him. "It won't be easy, but I've made a start. And that's down to you."

"I'm so glad. But could you tell me one thing? Just what is that tattoo on your arm?"

Kieran looked down at the winged sword. "Oh, that. It's the SAS."

Street of Ghosts by Josie Elson

Gerry watched the grey mist slither from the surface of the River Trent and make its way across the fields and railway sidings. It curled its way down passages and in between buildings, gradually unfurling before it came to rest like a shroud across the High Street.

He stood by the gates of the level crossing. He listened again to the rock-n-roll music blasting out of the Mocambo Coffee Bar opposite the shoe factory. He waited just as he had done for the last fifty years, on the same night of every one of those years. The Anniversary.

He still wore his black drainpipe trousers and Teddy Boy coat with its black velvet collar. It was long, almost to his knees. In a vivid cobalt blue, it matched his suede crepe-soled shoes. He had made a special effort, as always. The finishing touch was his black hair slicked back into a fashionable D A.

He knew by heart what would happen next. He turned to look past the sweet shop where he worked, towards the post office. He edged forward to gaze along the railway track that ran across the road. This was part of an internal network that transported trucks bearing barrels and other items from one brewery yard to another.

Soon a bell would clang to warn road users that the gates were going to open. The road would be closed while the trucks made their way across.

Once again Gerry peered anxiously towards the post office. Any minute the small side door would open and a bicycle would appear and Pat would push it to the edge of the pavement.

Was there nothing he could do to change what he knew was about to happen? He tried to distract the signalman in the box, but he ignored him as always and sounded the bell. When the traffic stopped, the man furiously turned the wheel that opened the gates.

Looking again towards the post office, Gerry could see Pat with her left foot on the pedal, scooting along to gather speed before she drew her right leg through the frame of her cycle.

He knew she had heard the bell. She glanced neither right nor left as she made her way towards him. He stood in her path, waving his arms to attract her attention. She rode straight through him. Once again he heard the sound of the cars as they hooted their warnings.

As always he watched in horror as she bent her head low and with skirt and coat flapping behind her, she pedalled frantically towards the ever-decreasing gap as the gates came together. Pat was in a race to get through before they clicked into place, barring her way while the trucks clattered unimpeded across the road.

On other nights she would have waited but on this night, the anniversary night, she was in a hurry and Gerry knew why.

How he wished he had not sent that anonymous note, the one purporting to be from someone who said he was the man of her dreams, the one she was waiting for. Curiosity compelled her to hurry. She wanted to see who this perfect man could be. Was it who she hoped it would be?

Gerry hadn't signed the note thinking it would be thrown away. He had always known that Pat's friends laughed at him, but he felt it was because they didn't know him. Pat would come into the shop for sweets or chocolate and they would stand outside, giggling. He became tongue-tied and he would catch Pat smiling. He thought that if they could meet somewhere other than the shop, she might start to see him differently.

So she was hurrying to meet this man of her dreams in the coffee bar. To her it was an adventure and it seemed she was prepared to take chances to get there on time.

Without stopping she hurtled through the gap just as she had every anniversary night for the last fifty years. Gerry was forced to watch as the back wheel of her cycle was caught in the heavy gates. Now, as then, it was too late to stop the engine and its trail of trucks. The bike was buckled beyond repair and Pat's life was lost yet again.

At last the engine and its trucks screeched to a

halt. The mist rose higher and thicker. The gates remained closed, blocking the road. Gerry walked through them just as he had all those years ago. He left his body under the wheels of the car that had struck him as he attempted to stop Pat on her whirlwind ride to oblivion.

He bent down and offered her a helping hand. She pushed him away and after standing erect for a minute, walked on down the street; she didn't look back or speak to him. She seemed to ignore him in death just as she had in life.

He stood up and watched her walk towards the coffee bar. On other anniversaries he had hidden his feelings but this year tears were stinging his eyes and trickling down his face, hopelessness was taking over.

Without warning Pat stopped and looked back. She must have seen his distress for her own face became distorted and it crumpled as she carried on walking.

The expression on her features had been fleeting, lasting only seconds, but Gerry had seen it; it gave him hope and he followed her. Could this be the year when he would finally be able to make her listen to his declaration of love?

As he entered the coffee bar the mist was beginning to slink back to the river. The street shivered and the shoe factory and the rail tracks were starting to disappear. Time was running out.

Gerry looked across the tables. Pat was drinking coffee, a puzzled look on her face. He decided to tell her about the note. He rested his hand on hers and was surprised when she locked her fingers into his.

Gently he told her about his trick with the letter.

"I regretted it as soon as I'd sent it but I was desperate. I just wanted a chance to tell you that I love you."

He tightened his grip on her fingers afraid she would let go. Gerry looked down at her. Pat's head was bent forward and her hair fell over her face, so he didn't see the smile that slowly lit up her eyes. When she finally looked at him her features glowed with such happiness he began to hope his dream was coming true at last.

Merriment made her eyes flash. She spoke so quietly he had to lower his head close to hers.

"Everyone told me that I shouldn't be too obvious about my feelings; that I should wait for you to make the first move. I didn't really want the chocolate I bought. It was just an excuse to come in the shop; I always gave it away. I thought you were never going to tell me how much you cared. I wanted so much to hear you say it out loud. When I got the note I hoped it was from you."

He clutched her hands so tightly she thought they would break and then he drew them close to him.

"I've been a fool haven't I?"

She nodded. "We both have."

They stood and held each other close.

Outside the mist had almost completely disappeared back to where it came from. The 1960's ghostly street was hazy and indistinct. The coffee bar gave way to a kebab shop.

Gerry and Pat were still clinging to one another as their spirits drifted away with the mist.

From now on their anniversaries wouldn't be a terrifying ordeal with only pain and heartbreak.

From this time forward it would be a celebration and they would go straight to the coffee bar, drink coffee together and dance to rock-n-roll music for all eternity.

Low-lights by Maggs Payne

I sit alone in the bar going over the day's events. It had all started with my visit to the hairdressers...

"Are-you-alright-then?" She always greets me like this does Sharon; never waits for an answer. We were at school together. Her mum owned the salon then and Sharon worked Saturdays and holidays. 'Shaz', that's what my mates and I called her if we wanted to wind her up.

"Must be nice to have a mommy who can afford to buy anything you want! You might have designer hot pants, but with a rear like that you would look better in a sack. Those white stretch boots would look much better on me." She was a great lump in those days. How I envied her those boots!

Shaz retaliated, "I work every Saturday and school holidays in the salon to earn my money."

We were all jealous of her spending power. One time we asked, "Shaz would you like to come to a rave up on Saturday at the Village Hall?" Actually, the party was to be held on the Friday at Lynda's house.

Saturday evening I said, "Let's watch her from behind the bushes opposite the village hall."

"I feel a bit mean, she's crying," one of my mates whinges.

I did have a twinge of conscience. "Yeah, well serves her right. It's not our fault she's got the days and venue muddled up."

Shaz stopped crying and shouted, "You lot behind the bushes, you're all bullies, especially you June/Juliet, whatever you call yourself. One day I'll get even with you!"

"Going to put a hex on me, dumpling?" I challenged.

That was years ago, long forgotten by me. Sharon does my hair every week. She often comments, "The past is in the past Juliet."

I nod my head at her reflection in the mirror, unsure to what she is referring. All that said, she's a good hairdresser. These days her mum only works part-time and Sharon runs the show. I wouldn't dream of going anywhere else. No, 'Lighten-Up' is the best salon in town.

I hand her a birthday card - '40 Today'. She's not amused! She places it at the back of the other cards and sulks. "There's no need to let everyone know my age!" Sharon's not known for her eloquence. She's all gold is Sharon; necklaces, chain-belts and God knows how many rings in her ears. She's an icon of faddy fashion. Every time her T-shirt rides up her gold studded navel's on display. Her slender wrists dangle with a charm bracelet.

"I'm meeting an old flame tonight," I tell her. "You remember Philip, my first love! Then I got pregnant by his best mate and that was my future sealed. A single mum at 17. I've never got over Philip. Took me to see South Pacific at the Palace Cinema. We sat in a double seat at the back."

"Another one on your hit list?" Sharon poses, consultant-like, then she advises me to have low-lights. "Knock years off you Juliet!"

To be honest my name's June, but I prefer Juliet. Love stories always have a Juliet don't they? I confide in Sharon. "Phil's phone call was a surprise. He's got an Australian accent, said his marriage ended in divorce. No children, so nothing to keep him there. He has a managerial job in London. Only here for the weekend catching up with old friends. I'd forgotten his parents moved to Skegness after Phil went abroad. We didn't stop talking, Sharon! He's visited them several times; strange he didn't get in touch before. Derby would be easy enough to break his journey to come and see me."

Two hours later I'm tonged and sprayed. Low-lighted, I see the new me. "Not bad for forty hey Sharon? I'm really pleased."

"You look years younger", she says wanting a tip. Her reflection takes on her consultant's persona. "You need a complete change of image Juliet. May I suggest nail extensions, red-gloss polish? Be a good idea to go to the boutique next door. They stock clothes, shoes and, of course, knee-length boots are the in-thing for the young-at-heart."

I succumb to her flattery and shop. The assistant selects various garments for me. "Let me help you try them on, then I can ensure your hair doesn't become messed up." Finally, she tells me "I think the red silk blouse with the red stiletto boots, worn with the tight, short, black skirt are definitely you. Why don't you go and show Sharon? Ask her opinion."

The bill will empty my bank account, but then Phil's worth it.

Sharon's face is a picture. "Juliet, you look...you look twenty years younger. Wasn't that about your age when you last saw him?" She smiles; actually it's more of a smirk. "Here," she says, handing me a small sealed envelope, "Not to be opened until after your evening is over. May it be a happy one!"

On my way out to meet Phil I pop into my daughter's. "Mum you look...you must be out of..."

"Is it fancy dress, Nanna?" my three year old granddaughter asks.

My heels clack on the tiled pub floor trying to bridge the twenty year gap. As I cross the room I can almost hear '*One Enchanted Evening*'.

Phil's at the bar. I recognise his face in the mirrored wall - life's lines etched against his Australian tan. He looks good. He looks at me, I wave. He comes over to me.

"June you look different. Sorry I didn't recognise you, then twenty years is a long time and no doubt the years have taken their toll on me too."

He doesn't make eye contact with me. Is he saying I've aged a lot? No, he's obviously dazzled by my new outfit. He puts his hand in his pocket and almost immediately his mobile rings.

"Sorry, need to take this call." He finishes his brief conversation. "Sorry again June, it's an emergency. Be in touch." He makes a hasty exit.

I know the call was a set-up. Perhaps I wasn't quite what he was expecting.

My feet take me to the nearest table. Tears sting my eyes. Taking a tissue from my new red handbag, my hand touches the envelope Sharon gave me.

"June/Juliet, I have waited a long time to take my revenge. This time I led and you followed me up the virtual garden path. My boutique assistant – yes, the boutique became mine yesterday – followed my instructions to dress you as if you were going to a Vicar and Tarts party. Your backside looked enormous in that tight black skirt."

Her final paragraph reads: *"If the goods you purchased from my boutique are in pristine condition your money will be refunded, but not the boots!"*

Memories fill my head and shame is my companion now. Yet another low-light in my life!

Long-term Planning by Mary Gladstone

Beth heard the swish of tyres as her brother-in-law's car pulled up at the front door of the beautiful old farmhouse and her heart sank. Peter was 'something in the city'. Something shady thought Beth irritably, and then she heard the strident, cut-glass voice of his wife.

"I hope they've put the heating on this time. I would have preferred to stay in a hotel. I did tell you so."

Beth couldn't hear Peter's murmured reply.

The car door slammed and there was a peremptory hammering on the front door. Beth pressed her hands against the cold, smooth porcelain of the kitchen sink. Her eyes welled with tears of anger, frustration and sadness. "I refuse to play housemaid to those two this time - Pops has gone and I don't have to try and keep the peace. Let them knock." She sat down heavily.

Pops dead. Dear Pops who had still taken part in the milking every morning at six o'clock even though he was eighty-two, until a week ago when he hadn't come down to breakfast. Then everything had changed.

Her husband Rob was the second son and until now had managed the farm. Would he soon be looking for another job together with their sons?

They had already received offers as they were well known in the farming community, but they loved this rambling old house and all it stood for.

The farm, lock, stock and barrel, would be inherited by Peter, the eldest son. It had always been so for over three hundred years. Certainly, a sad time was coming.

The hammering continued on the front door. Beth sighed and stood up.

"Let them knock, or come around the back."

"What?" Beth was startled out of her reverie and turned toward the voice. Lizzie was standing by the oven, tiny fists on tiny waist, timeless old Lizzie, who had helped in the house and dairy since Beth had arrived as a young bride over thirty years ago. She had been Beth's guide, confidante and friend.

"You are not their servant. You are still mistress of this house and they are family, not royalty. Let them knock or come around the back." Lizzie smiled her gappy grin. "Let it go, be yourself, speak up. There's no need to be nervous of those two."

"I am not," Beth insisted but knew she was lying because Fiona, real name Doris as they discovered on her wedding day, always seemed to wrong-foot her. And Peter was so dismissive in his attitude towards her that even against her will she found herself trying to please.

"Accept what is and let all else go," Lizzie repeated.

Beth took a deep breath. "Indeed, why should I let those two townies undermine me? Where's my backbone?"

The back door crashed open and a very irate Fiona stood framed in the doorway, her face suffused with fury.

"Why didn't you open the front door? You must have heard me knocking. Look at my shoes, they're ruined."

"What silly shoes to wear on a country visit," said Beth calmly. "Haven't you any decent brogues?"

"I wouldn't need dreadful brogues if you had bothered to open the door." Fiona scowled.

"Not good enough you know Beth, old thing," chided Peter quietly as he stepped into the kitchen and kissed her perfunctorily on the cheek.

Beth caught Lizzie's eye and bit back the apology which was rising to her lips through habit.

"Is there anything to eat? I'm starving." Peter sank into a chair at the kitchen table, leaned back and looked hopefully at Beth.

"I'm not eating in the kitchen." Fiona glared at Beth. "We'll eat in the dining room like civilised people." It was a definite instruction.

"Well, take those shoes off before you track mud through," said Beth, "and keep the place tidy for the wake tomorrow. As for food there's plenty in the fridge and larder. Just help yourselves."

Peter looked surprised. "Just sort a few bits and pieces for us Beth, and bring it through. We've driven up from Town and are quite tired. A couple of salads will do, the cheese board and biscuits, that sort of thing. Nothing fancy and has Rob got any decent wine in?" Peter smiled his most engaging smile and went through to the dining room to placate Fiona.

Beth sighed and stood up, defeated, but Lizzie intervened.

"We should check the cloths and glasses for tomorrow," she said with determination, "and cast a quick eye over the lounge and conservatory. I think everything is OK but people might be arriving quite early and we still have the farm to run."

"You are quite right Lizzie, as usual, and let's take a couple of glasses of that rather nice Chardonnay to help oil our wheels."

Lizzie and Beth stood by the lounge window and watched the sun set on the glorious view.

"How appropriate," said Beth, "I love this house, the farm and the life. Now everything must change. That's bad enough, but we have always understood the terms. The worst thing is I know they won't look after it."

They heard footsteps and like children hid their wine behind the curtain and were busily flicking dusters around when Fiona burst into the room.

"We are still waiting for our meal," she grated.

"Well I told you where the food was," said Beth, "and 'them that wants can step and fetch' as my mother used to say. We don't run a waitress service here."

"After tomorrow I will be making some changes," threatened Fiona.

"Well I won't be here to see them, will I?" snapped Beth.

She turned and looked out of the window

again. Rob was slowly crossing the bottom paddock, head down, his two collies walking close at his heels, glancing up at him as though understanding his sadness and wishing to give comfort.

She walked down to meet him, slipped her arm through his and tried to be cheerful. "Peter and Fiona have arrived."

He glanced quizzically at her. "Well they'll be ruling the roost from tomorrow, no mistake."

"They've already started," said Beth ruefully.

Rob laughed and pulled her arm more tightly through his. "We'll be alright love."

"I know." She smiled.

Beth rose early the next morning. As expected the dining table was littered with dirty dishes and scraps of food, the air filled with stale smoke. As she opened windows and cleared the table she began to fume inwardly again. Lizzie's words came back to her: 'Accept what is' and she felt calmer.

Pop's funeral was to be at eleven-thirty and guests started to arrive shortly after ten. Fiona and Peter just hung around in the background making no effort to meet and greet until a particular gentleman arrived whom Beth didn't know. They watched him like hawks as he strolled around the rooms, hands clasped behind his back. When the three of them slipped into the study Beth quite shamelessly listened at the door. The stranger was speaking. "...are very nice. The silver is excellent. The furniture is well used but should still be worth quite a bit."

"I hope so," said Peter, "because we need the money and the sale should set us up for life. I will also be selling some of the land, but I want to try to get planning permission first to increase the value."

"Well, of course I can't comment on that. Not my province, but it is sad to see these old family places break up. How long did you say your family has been here?"

"Over three hundred years. Time for a change I say." Peter laughed.

"And we need the money," cut in Fiona.

Beth moved away from the door. She felt dizzy with shock. They are going to break the place up. Sell it off piecemeal. She couldn't tell Rob, not today of all days. It would destroy him.

The funeral guests had left. The family sat around the large dining table with Mr. Turnbull their solicitor and Lizzie, who was always included in any family event. Village gossip had it that Mr. Turnbull, Lizzie and Pops had been a very troublesome trio in their youth, into all sorts of scrapes and mischief. Hard to imagine it now, but there was a definite bond between them. Lizzie had always been a law unto herself and lived in one of the farm cottages for a peppercorn rent.

Mr. Turnbull steepled his slender white fingers and waited.

"Oh get on with it," said Peter testily. "When can I take over and what's it worth. I know the terms of the will."

"Well," replied Mr. Turnbull slowly, "except for a few small legacies everything goes to Rob."

The silence was almost tangible.

"Rob? Rob! But it's mine," spluttered Peter, "always has been. This is illegal. I'll fight it in the Courts. *They,*" he pointed to Rob and Beth, "manipulated him in his dotage. We all know he was becoming senile. Three hundred years of tradition can't be overturned just like that."

"You'll lose," replied the solicitor calmly. "This will was made over twenty-five years ago when you left the farm for London. You borrowed £50,000 to set up a business."

"I remember that," interrupted Rob bitterly. "We had to sell two cottages to raise that amount."

Mr. Turnbull continued to answer Peter as though Rob hadn't spoken.

"You signed a loan agreement."

"Well so what? The money was going to come to me anyway."

"The contract you signed, which your father advised you most seriously to read, stipulated that if the loan - with nominal interest - was not settled prior to your father's death your rights under the existing will would be forfeit, and the whole of your entitlement would return to the estate. You borrowed using your expected inheritance as collateral and defaulted. Since then you have borrowed more and more until the final amount is some £250,000. As you haven't repaid it your right to the farm has been taken in settlement of the debt."

Visibly shaken, Peter sat white lipped. "The old fox. Lead me right up the garden path and no mistake."

"Using your greed as bait," agreed Mr. Turnbull.

"But how much do we get?" asked Fiona.

"Nothing. Your husband sold his birthright," replied Mr. Turnbull.

"It can't be legal," whispered Peter, "it can't

be."

"I assure you it's watertight," said Mr. Turnbull. "Tom knew you weren't interested in the farm, only the money. He also knew Rob and Beth will continue to work it and eventually hand it on. Perhaps the family will hold it for another three hundred years."

The truth was beginning to dawn on Fiona. "We get nothing?"

"You get a £250,000 debt paid," said Mr. Turnbull blandly.

Fiona and Peter left noisily complaining, "You haven't heard the last of this."

Beth and Rob hugged each other. Blossom Farm was theirs. Their home and their future were safe.

As they left the room Beth glanced back. Was it a trick of the light or did she really see old Mr. Turnbull and Lizzie exchange a high five? Surely not, but she secretly hoped she had.

The Sign by Barbara Swallow

On the morning Bill woke to find that his garden had disappeared over the edge of the cliff, he made a decision. He wouldn't move. He'd sit in his home and wait. If the good Lord wanted him to move, he'd send him a sign.

"Don't you think he's done that already, sending your garden down to the beach?" Ruby asked as she spread a green and white checked tablecloth on her father's kitchen table. "Or are you expecting him to reach down and give you a push?"

"Don't be ridiculous. He's got more on his mind at the moment."

"So have I," Ruby replied. "I've a family and a farm to see to in case you've forgotten." She got cutlery out of the dresser drawer and banged it down on the cloth. "I've done my best to get you to move back with us but if you don't want to then you'll have to stay put." She went into the sitting room, slamming the kitchen door behind her.

The cottage wobbled on its foundations and Bill held his breath. He'd got used to the movements going on in the ground underneath him. He found something quite soothing about the slight rocking motion of his home. But he was glad Ruby still drove out to the headland every day to bring his dinner. He was her father after all, even if he was a daft old man, but he knew her patience had begun to wear thin and she was worried about him.

"Dad, I'm bringing the vet to see you tomorrow," she said as she came back into the kitchen and put his dinner to warm.

"The vet? Why? Are you planning to have me put down?"

"Don't be daft, I mean Henry."

Henry had been the vet all the time Bill had run the farm. Both men had retired in the same year but he was still referred to as the vet by the locals. The two old friends had regularly met in the Hare and Hounds to have a drink, a chat and a game of chess. That was until Bill decided to 'stay put'.

"He's just coming to have a talk."

"What sort of a talk?"

"Just a friendly one. Maybe give you a bit of advice."

"Ah, advice! He was always good at that."

"You used to listen to him. You certainly don't listen to me." Ruby slammed the door behind her as she left. And Bill steadied himself, waiting for the floor to stop vibrating.

The next day, Henry arrived as Ruby was bringing Bill's dinner - beef stew and dumplings in a big brown pot. The vet eyed it hungrily. Unlike Bill, he hadn't a family to take care of him. He was dependant on the vagaries of his housekeeper whose cooking was not was a good as Ruby's.

"Are you going to join me then Henry?" Bill asked, laying two places at the table.

The vet sat down, picked up a knife and fork, and watched eagerly as Bill ladled out the stew.

The two men ate in silence. Good food needed no conversation in their opinion. Seconds were had and the dish scraped round before Henry sat back with a happy sigh.

Bill produced some bottles of beer and they went through to the sitting room.

The vet frowned. Was it his imagination or did the floor sway a little as they walked across it?

They set up the chess board. After a while and a few more bottles of beer, they noticed something rather odd. The chess pieces were moving all by themselves. The beer gone, they found a bottle of scotch at the back of the cupboard. They drank as they watched the knights, instead of their usual dog-legged canter, gallop straight down the board. The rooks careered after them, followed, in a more dignified fashion, by the bishops. The King and Queen, together until the end, were the last to leave the board and slid to the carpet to join the other pieces.

"I won," shouted Henry, waving his arms about.

"Rubbish, I won," shouted Bill. The argument went fiercely on until the two friends began to giggle. They slumped in their chairs and their laughter turned to snores as the sky darkened.

When Ruby came to collect the dishes, for a moment she thought it looked like a suicide pact. Two prostrate bodies, empty bottles and glasses and chessmen scattered about the room. She stacked the dishes in her basket and left the vet where he was. She couldn't be responsible for everything. The door slammed behind her as she went out and the cottage moved a little more.

By the time the two men woke up, rain was pouring down outside, washing away at the foundations.

"You can't walk home in this, Henry," Bill protested as the vet put his coat on.

"No problem, I've got my bike." He gave a cheerful, unsteady wave and wobbled up the road.

The next day when Ruby arrived she banged the dish down on the table. "What do you two think you were doing yesterday?"

Bill winced. "Having a chat, like you said."

"I didn't tell you to pour beer down the vet's throat. I don't suppose you heard but he was found fast asleep in a ditch with his bike on top of him."

"Mm, never did have much of a head for drink. And he lost at chess."

Ruby stormed out and the cottage moved again. Bill stood and considered the horizon through the window. Did the floor slope more than usual? He hadn't had a drink today. Not after yesterday.

The rain continued to come down. There seemed no end to it. Bill found he spent more and more time pushing his armchair back up the room as it continually gravitated towards the window.

Ruby became alarmed. Her plump face creased with worry as she said: "Dad, you have to move."

"I haven't had a sign yet."

"Isn't your home moving to the edge of the cliff sign enough?"

But the old man refused to budge.

"Dad, I'm going to bring the vicar round."

"What's he going to do? Perform a miracle?"

Ruby's eyes filled with tears. "I'm just trying to help. Maybe he can talk some sense into you. No one else can."

"I know you are love and I'm being what I am, a stubborn old man."

After his daughter had left, Bill wondered if he was being selfish. He felt old and tired. Perhaps it was time to let fate take a hand? Then he laughed at himself for being a pompous old fool.

The next day when Ruby and the vicar arrived, Bill refused to let them in. They hammered on the door and the cottage moved a little more. The vicar shouted a blessing through the letter-box, shook his head at Ruby and walked away. The wind wrapped his cassock round him, making him look like one of the ravens from the church tower. Perhaps he is, thought Bill as he watched them go. Perhaps he perches up there at night recording our sins.

Finally the night came when the storm surpassed itself. Rain, hail, thunder and lightning were unleashed on the inhabitants of the village. It was far worse out on the headland. Bill woke up and slid down the floor towards the window. The whole of his world was shaking. He looked out towards the sea and there in front of him was his garden path, the same one that weeks ago had fallen off the cliff.

"Now that's what I call a sign," he said and

smiled to himself. Climbing out of the window was easier than he'd imagined as it now touched the ground. He didn't hear the crash of falling stone walls as he slid out and began walking up the garden path.

Roses so Deeply Red by Josie Elson

The church was packed. The hum of subdued voices ceased as the coffin was guided forward. I walked beside it, resting my hand on the lid; the nearest I could get to holding his hand just one more time. Once again we were amid his precious flowers. Some of them adorned his coffin. Among them, a rose so deeply red it was almost black.

The hush was shattered as the door of the church opened to admit another mourner. The sound of his footsteps rebounded off the walls as he made his way to the bier. He laid a single red rose next to mine, a rose so deeply red it was almost black. As he turned he smiled at me. I beckoned for him to come and sit with the family. For just a moment our hands touched. He gave me an envelope and I looked at him properly for the first time. I pressed my hand across my chest in vain, trying to stop the drumming of my heart. He was the image of Alex.

"My mother loved him too. She understood

and she would have wished you both well," he said and sat beside me throughout the service, but once it was done he disappeared.

Leaving the church I realised I was still clutching the letter. My sons would want to know about the man who looked so like their father. They would be curious about the letter too, but today was not the day to reveal secrets.

I decided to read it later in the solitude of our–my-bedroom.

The gathering of friends and relatives dispersed and then there were just our sons and their families staying with me for a few days, which was a great comfort to me. All too soon school and work commitments meant they would have to leave me. I need to cope alone.

Alex had always prepared our bedtime drinks. We both liked to read for a while before we turned out the light. He would make the tea in a pot. Now it would be one teabag in a single cup. Somehow the bed looked bigger and I felt lost in it. I tossed and turned most of the night and at about 3 am I remembered the letter.

It was a brief note of condolence. The photograph with it spoke more eloquently than words ever could. On the back the inscription said: "Mother and father's wedding day". It was an unnecessary title. Alex and his bride Eva smiled out at me. The photograph was taken just a year or two before the war. He stood so proud and protective at his bride's side.

Alex had told me only a little of his life before coming to England and certainly he never mentioned his wife. When he left his oppressed country to join the fight for freedom he came here and trained as a pilot.

We met shortly after his training had ended. I was so proud of him in his pilot's uniform. I declared my love for him on many occasions but something seemed to be holding him back. Nothing I could say would tempt him to reveal his troubles. I dreaded the end of the war for it meant Alex would be going home.

When the conflict finally ended we heard that his homeland was now governed by a different regime just as oppressive as the last and his return home was still impossible. It was then Alex asked me in faltering English to marry him.

Dad was against the marriage. "He's a foreigner. You know nothing about him. You mark my words, my girl, he's leading you up the garden path."

And that's just what Alex did, every day of our married life. He would take my hand and lead me to the garden. We walked the paths together and I stared in wonder at his handiwork. His pride and joy were the roses he grew, so red they was almost black.

So here I am, mourning the death of this gentle man I loved so much. My father, who had distrusted him at the beginning, came to accept him as his own.

The irony of all this is that the Berlin Wall was torn down last November and although Alex was very ill he rejoiced in the freedom of the people. Part of me was glad that he was too ill to make the journey home, but my sadness at his illness helped to blot out my selfish thoughts. Now I am pleased I did not reveal to him that I knew his secret.

Newly married and curious I had dared to look into his memory box. Underneath many mementoes I found a copy of the same photograph the man in the church had given me.

The only letter Alex received from Eva was there too. It was dog-eared and stained. It had obviously been read many times. I could only imagine the heartbreak he must have felt each time he looked at it.

I sit in bed with this new letter; I cry the tears I ought to have shed for him then. At the time I was angry but slowly I came to recognise the anguish he must have endured. He would have been afraid to tell me of his other family fearing I would reject him. I made a choice. I would keep quiet.

I am again facing difficult choices. Do I tell our sons? If so, do I tell them everything? Do I tell them they have a brother?

It was a long night with no sleep. I was at the kitchen table with a cup of coffee when Ethan appeared; Daniel was still in bed enjoying a rare lie in.

Ethan filled his cup and joined me at the table. He nodded towards the letter. "Going to tell me about him then, Mum? Who was he? Dad's younger brother, nephew, cousin...son?"

He stared at me and I felt sure he already knew the answer. I handed him the envelope. "Son," I said.

"Bit of a dark horse was he then, our dad?"

By this time Daniel had appeared. It had to be now or I would never do it. I plunged straight in.

"Dad was already married when we met. He

had a wife and a son living behind the iron curtain. I only found out after we married, but it wouldn't have made any difference. I would have married him anyway." It was a relief to get the truth out.

"I never told your father that I knew his secret. Why sour my relationship with a good and loving man? He could never go back and now the destruction of the Berlin Wall has come too late for him. At least he was spared the torment of choosing between us and his first family."

I stopped talking to allow them time to absorb the news and all its implications. The silence was breaking my heart but I had to give them a little more time.

Ethan spoke first, "Dad was a great bloke. It seems to me he made the best life he could for both of you in the circumstances."

Daniel nodded his agreement and added, "Mum, you were right not to tell him you knew his secret. There was no point in breaking both your hearts. But this Eva you mentioned, you say she died some time ago. How did their son know that dad had died?"

"When your father became ill I traced his son and wrote to him, but I think travel restrictions prevented him from coming. Since then the Wall has been demolished and things are easier."

Ethan gave me one of his enquiring looks. "This half brother of ours, he's a bit short on family then?"

"That's about it. He flies home in a few days."

Daniel and Ethan looked at each other.

"Well," said Daniel, "perhaps we should throw a little party to welcome him to this one."

I could have kissed them both but they would have hated it.

Luka arrived at my door two days later. With a little bow he handed me a single rose, it matched the ones we had placed side by side on his father's coffin.

The Key by Maggs Payne

Overbridge Hall in Derbyshire, empty since 1945, is to be demolished; we are going to watch its demise. "A chance to lay a few ghosts, Jenny!" Peter's quip sounds ominous; on that last day he wasn't involved, I was responsible and I have the key to prove it.

The key is cold against my hand. Fifty two years ago I stole the key - the last day of our evacuation. Sometimes I convince myself that I was unable to turn the huge key in the lock. I am haunted by these thoughts.

To my husband, Jim, my children and grandchildren, I am reliable, caring Jenny. They don't know I carry this dark secret.

My twin brother, Peter, and I celebrated our 60th birthdays two weeks ago. I look in the mirror: my hair, once the colour of burnished copper, has faded. The sun, streaming in through the window, highlights my blonde streaks. A touch of blusher and pink lipstick adds colour to my pale appearance. I'm waiting for him to arrive. We have planned a trip down 'memory lane'.

Peter's Mercedes smells of polished leather. Am I more nervous than I was as a six year old? He doesn't talk much throughout the fifty mile journey. This gives my mind the opportunity to make its own journey. I try to keep my thoughts on today. His hair has faded too; the grey threaded through it gives him a distinguished appearance. His eyes reflect my own, dark brown with hazel flecks. With each mile my memories become more vivid.

****

In 1943, after sitting for three hours in a bone-shaker of a charabanc, we arrived at the village hall somewhat bedraggled. The winter afternoon was darkening as the Welfare lady drove us up a wide pathway between an avenue of trees. Their dark branches casting shadows made me scared. I held Peter's hand as we entered Overbridge Hall. In the kitchen we were greeted by the smell of carbolic soap; through a cloud of steam we could make out a slight figure bending over a washtub.

She whispered, "I'm Cissy and you must be the evacuees, you poor little ducks."

The Welfare lady spoke slowly, "Cissy dear, go and fetch Mrs. Grafton. Do say I am in a hurry. I have other children to take to their foster homes."

Cissy scuttled off as if her life depended on it.

The Welfare lady explained to us, "Most of the Hall is closed down and Cissy is the only help to be kept on."

The kitchen door opened. Through the clammy steam appeared Cissy, accompanied by a large woman who wore a black dress. Her huge bosom rested on a wide black leather belt around her non-existent waist. Hanging from the belt were several keys, so that she clanked as she walked. Later we learned one of the keys was for the door from our bedroom into a secret sound-proofed room.

The Welfare lady introduced us to Mrs. Grafton. "Jenny and Peter are orphans; their parents were killed in a bombing raid two years ago. They've been living with their grandmother, their only relative. Sadly she is very ill in hospital. Mrs. Grafton, I understand that you live alone? Taking in two evacuees may be difficult for you. However, war makes demands of everyone. I can assure you that Jenny and Peter have excellent reports from their school."

Mrs. Grafton spoke, "You're both welcome. I will take good care of you." Her voice was kind and not at all scary.

The Welfare lady said, "I will visit in two weeks time." I felt tears stinging my eyes as she said, "Goodbye children."

"Cissy, get them bathed and straight to bed." Mrs. Grafton's voice changed, it was as black as her dress. "They don't need any supper, the Welfare ladies fed them at the Village Hall."

Peter complained, "We're starving, we've only had cocoa and a biscuit."

Mrs. Grafton bellowed, "One more complaint and you won't have any breakfast either. Cissy! Upstairs with them I don't want to hear another sound; a good scrubbing is what they need. You two don't speak unless I speak to you first and stop that snivelling."

Cissy ran a few inches of water into an old metal bath that stood regally on claw-like feet; there were green stains below the taps. The room was so cold ice covered the inside of the window. We sat either end of the bath and Cissy proceeded to wash us with a soapy flannel.

She told us, "I was your age when I came here as an orphan. They fostered me. It was such a happy place. Mrs. Grafton shut herself off when her husband and their little girl were killed in an accident. I do my best, twenty six years I've been here and I would never leave her."

Cissy had left us in our nightclothes ready for bed when Mrs. Grafton clanked up the stairs, walked into our bedroom and pressed a notch in the panelling. This sprung open revealing a door that she unlocked and shoved me into complete darkness. Peter must have flung himself at her because he, too, was bundled into the blackness with me.

Her hands, with sausage-like fingers, were silhouetted against the gas light from the bedroom and she was clasping a bottle. "You will stay there until morning while I have a drink in peace." And she locked the door.

After all our tears for mummy, daddy and gran were shed we fell asleep on a rag rug that smelt of damp dogs.

We were woken before daylight; we were in our beds! How? Then a voice said, "Don't tell, my little ducks; this is our secret, back into that room with you."

Worse followed. After being at the Hall for a few weeks Mrs. Grafton told us that our gran had died.

"Our only visitor will be the Welfare lady, you know how to behave," she boomed.

Our hearts seemed to hurt constantly. We felt as if we were totally alone.

****

Peter and I never have discussed our time at the Hall or felt the need to return to the place of our two-year exile. After the war I began having horrendous nightmares. These have become infrequent as the years put distance between the past and me. What if this visit proves my nightmares to be reality? Finally, I decide witnessing the Hall crumble would indeed, 'lay a few ghosts'.

Peter interrupts my thoughts. "Have you been dozing Jenny? We're here!"

It is one of those spring days when summer promises to make an early appearance; a day of brightness and colour; crocus, daffodils and clusters of snowdrops on display. The grass glints with the moisture of the April frost, droplets of water lie on the petals of the spring flowers skirting the bottom of the trees. Are they the tears from our days of exile?

We park, take a short cut across the bridge over the river, walk along the grass verge to the entrance of Overbridge Hall. The avenue of trees is in full blossom. Had the sky ever been this blue or the perfume of spring so sweet? My memories of the Hall are of carbolic soap and maturing apples!

The builders have begun their demolition. Using binoculars I watch as the crane swings its metal ball suspended on a clanking metal chain. I shudder...the resounding thud is followed by the sound of falling debris and dust obliterates our view. Then before the crane swings into action again, I see the bedroom that we once shared.

Fifty two years ago my child's eyes saw it as a large, dark, forbidding room; I remember two small iron beds, the chest of drawers riddled with woodworm and a piano that we were forbidden to touch. I could almost smell the odour that had emanated from the apples stored behind the piano in an old wooden box.

The metal ball swings again, the dust clears and I see 'The Door'. Memories threaten to overwhelm me; I visualise the small room that lay beyond. As an eight year old child I could just reach to press the notch.

This small room became a dark threat in our young lives. The Witch, as we secretly called Mrs. Grafton, would ensure that we were put into the room for any misdemeanour. She told us, "All children who misbehave will go to hell." We came to think of the room as hell!

We discovered that she kept a crate of gin in the room. On many occasions we were taken out of the room, placed in our beds and returned to the room before The Witch stirred from her drunken stupor. She acted the jailer with so much confidence she didn't hide the opening and closing system of the panelling.

One day I asked Cissy, "How do you get us out of the room when the door is locked?" She clutched something in her apron pocket, "That's my secret little ducky."

The village school offered some respite. We were treated kindly. Each day The Witch gave us a cheese sandwich and an apple for our lunch. When we got home in the afternoon we had, on alternate days, corned beef hash and stew with plump dumplings. Cissy made sure we had enough to eat. The Witch told us, "You must not talk about me or Overbridge Hall, you know what will happen!"

Every fortnight the Welfare lady paid a visit. Cissy served tea and cake in the reception room. She kept the rooms that were in use polished and tidy. We were always on our best behaviour.

Towards the end of two years of unhappiness The Witch told us, "I have received a letter from the authorities informing me that a great-aunt of yours has been traced and is coming to take you home with her. What a relief, now with you two off my hands I can close the Hall and go where I want for as long as I want." We were overjoyed with the news.

The next morning we packed our belongings into small brown cardboard cases. The Witch said, "Sit on the settee, smile and mind your manners." Our great-aunt arrived and Mrs. Grafton greeted her warmly, "They are well-behaved children and have lived through so much sadness."

Great aunt smelt of lavender, she gave us a hug. I felt comforted when she told us, "You are part of my family now." Outside her car was waiting.

Peter shouted, "Wow! A Rolls". The driver showed Peter around the car and let him sit in his seat. Mrs. Grafton came out to wave us goodbye. The inside of the car smelt of polished leather. As we started off I said, "I'm so sorry great aunt I have forgotten my slippers."

I went back into the house. "Mrs. Grafton has gone upstairs," Cissy said, "I will miss you both."

"Cissy, what will happen to you now the Hall is to be closed?"

"I've been offered a job in the village pub where I will live in. Now don't go fretting about me, Jenny."

I crept quietly up the stairs. The Witch was just entering the secret room. I held my breath and noticed the key was in the door. Quickly I shut the door to the secret room and turned the key in the lock...

Mrs. Grafton shouted, "Who's there? Who's there? Who's..." I pressed the notch and the panel sprung back into place. It was now impossible for anyone to hear her cries.

I took the key and collected my slippers. Cissy was on the landing, one hand in her apron pocket. "Goodbye my little ducky. Don't worry, I will look after things."

****

We stand in the spring sunshine and watch our ghosts fall amongst the rubble of Overbridge Hall.

A Negative Answer by Barbara Swallow

"Come on you two. They can't hold up the train just for you."

May and Iris fell into the carriage, collapsing in a giggling heap opposite their mother. Mrs. Carter straightened her hat and looked disapprovingly at her youngest daughter.

"Iris, I thought I told you not to wear that dress today, it's too tight. I think you've grown out of it."

May glared at her sister. "I think Ma's right. You look a bit like a pint in a half pint pot."

May was small and thin like her father but Iris had inherited Ma's imposing figure.

"Where's Pa?" Iris asked, trying to divert attention from her size.

"Where do you think? He followed the beer into the next carriage."

"Oh Ma, he'll smell of beer all day." May pulled a face, but her mother glared at her.

"Don't let me hear you talking about your father like that my girl. It's his outing. He works hard all year and deserves at bit of pleasure."

May sighed. She knew her mother was right. The Bass outing was the high spot of his summer. Five trains full of Bass employees and their families had left Burton and were on their way to Scarborough

"Can we bathe in the sea, Ma?" Iris asked.

"No! It's not decent, taking all your clothes off in front of everyone." She straightened her hat again.

"Not all of them Ma, we wouldn't take them all off," Iris said.

"I said no. Now let's have a bit of peace to enjoy the journey. It's not every day we get a train ride as far as this." Mrs. Carter sat back to watch the passing scene through the window. Eventually her eyes closed and her head nodded forwarded onto her chest. That left the girls free to chatter to one another. They had plans that didn't include their parents.

Scarborough station was full of Bass coopers, brewers and other allied workers along with their families dressed in their best clothes. Everyone was looking forward to a day by the sea, despite the storm clouds gathering across Europe in the summer of 1914. The Carter family stood on the platform. Mr. Carter was a little shorter than his imposing wife but still liked to think of himself as head of the family and in charge. Mrs. Carter allowed him to believe so.

"Right now," he began addressing wife and daughters as if at a public meeting.

"Oh Lor, he's going to make a speech," Iris muttered, earning herself a slap on the arm from her mother.

Ignoring the interruption, Mr. Carter continued, "You two girls can go on the sands for an hour, then join us for some dinner. Your mother and I'll be in the Fisherman's Arms."

"Lucky old you." Iris earned herself another slap from her mother.

Together, the girls watched as their parents stroll along the harbour then they turned and ran in the direction of the beach.

"Right," Iris gasped as they ran down the steps, "get your costume on in that hut over there." They scampered into the bathing hut, pulling their costumes from their bags. May had bought them in the market and, unfortunately, they were all one size. She was covered from chin to knee in her red and white suit but Iris had more to fit in.

"Cover yourself up," May hissed at her sister as they stepped out into the sunshine

Iris looked down. "It's covering my knees."

"It's not your knees I'm worrying about. You're overflowing at the top. What would Ma say?"

Iris pulled hard on the woollen material. There was a noise of cracking stitches. "It won't stretch anymore. Anyway, Ma's not going to see."

They ran down to the sea, squealing as the cold water covered their feet.

"I'm not going any further," May said, the North Sea up to her knees. "Look, I'm going blue!"

Iris looked at her sister; perhaps she was going a bit purple in places. She grabbed her hand and they raced back up the beach. They stood quite still whilst they got their breath, heads back, looking into the sun. As Iris turned she thought she saw a flash.

"Thank you ladies," a voice called from the promenade. A young man was putting a plate into his bag and folding up his tripod.

"Hey," Iris shouted, "what do you think you're doing?"

"What I hope I've done is take your photographs. I've finished now. You were my last plate, I can pack up for the day."

"You can't do that," wailed May as he slipped the plate into his bag and slung his camera over his shoulder.

"But I just have. You'll be in Mr. Turner's shop window by the weekend." He gave them a cheery wave and walked off. Iris began to run after him but May pulled her back.

"You can't go chasing him up the promenade, you haven't any clothes on."

Already someone had turned to stare at the sight of two girls on their own running along the path. Iris screamed and dived back into the bathing hut. It took them ten minutes to change and hide their costumes in their bags. By the time they reached the promenade there was no sign of the photographer.

"We'd better find Ma and Pa before they start wondering what we've been doing," said May. "Mind you, they'll know soon enough once that picture goes in the window. Pa always looks in there to see what's been happening in the town."

Iris looked at her sister, who worked in the milliner's shop next door to the photographer's.

"Don't suppose you could go round to see Mr. Turner, could you?"

"You suppose right. Even if Miss Jones gave me the time off, I don't think Mrs. Turner would let me have a word. He's always in the dark room and she doesn't allow anyone in there with him."

Reaching the Fisherman's Arms, they paused to work up the courage to enter.

"Look!" Iris shouted.

May turned and saw the photographer going through the door into the bar. He gave them a cheeky wave as he went in. Iris went to follow but May pulled her back. "Wait a minute, then go and see where everyone is sitting."

"Why? Have you got an idea?"

"Don't know yet. Wait and see."

They slipped through the door and stood quietly at the back of the room. Their parents were down at the other end, talking to friends. The photographer had slid into a booth by the door, his case and tripod was on the floor at the side.

May looked at her sister. "Can you distract him for a moment?"

"How?"

"Shouldn't be too difficult." May pointed at Iris's tight dress. "Have a go."

Iris began walking towards her parents. As she reached the photographer's booth her feet seemed to tangle up in the strap of his bag. She fell across the table. He tried to catch her and trapped his hands beneath her soft, round body.

Whilst they were both saying how sorry they were but not moving, May gently slid the black case along the floor and round the corner of the booth towards the door.

She'd watch carefully when the man put the plate away and knew it was the one nearest the brass catch on the side of the bag. It was larger than she'd thought, making quite a bulge in her canvas bag. She pushed the case back just as the two on the table untangled themselves, both looking rather flushed.

May grabbed Iris's hand. "Come on, Ma and Pa will be waiting for us."

"I think I'll wait here a moment to recover," Iris said looking at the young man.

"No you won't! I don't want any more trouble today, thank you." She pushed her sister in the direction of their parents.

After dinner Ma stood up and smoothed down her dress. "Right, I think we three can go and look round the town. Pa's staying here. Then you can have one last sight of the sea before we go home."

May was conscious of the heavy plate in her bag as they wandered endlessly around the shops. She was relieved when Ma turned towards the harbour. They walked along the wall and looked at the boats tied up there. Making sure that Ma was talking to Iris, May slipped the plate out of her bag and dropped it gently into the water. She watched as it cockle-shelled its way down until it was lost from sight. Suddenly, feeling weak at the knees, she leant on the harbour wall.

"Are you alright, May?" Ma asked. "You've gone rather pale."

"Never better Ma." May pushed herself upright. She did feel alright now. "There's something about the sea that washes all your worries away."

Wanted: new man by Lynda Turner

Clad in his motorbike leathers Fred stomped into the kitchen. "I'll just change," he said.

"If only you would," mouthed Gemma under her breath as she heard him climb the stairs. She returned to her shopping list, sorely tempted to add *new man* beneath the groceries. List done, she went to the foot of stairs and shouted, "Nearly ready Fred?"

No reply.

She shouted again, waited a few moments then went after him. She entered the bedroom, halted and let out a loud gasp. "Fred! There's a big frog on our bed. Come and get rid of it now!"

No reply.

"Fred, where are you? If this is one of your practical jokes, it isn't funny!"

The frog croaked.

Gemma stepped around the creature and yanked the wardrobe door open. Fred's clothes hung there, but no Fred. "Are you hiding? Am I supposed to find you?" She made a big show of looking in all the usual places until, fed up, she collapsed onto the bed. "Okay, I give in, where are you?"

Throughout Gemma's performance the frog hadn't moved except for puffing out his throat and eyeballing her.

"What happens now?" She glared at him. "Croak once for yes and twice for no?"

It was meant to be a snide remark but, obligingly, the frog croaked once.

"Am I supposed to believe you're Fred?"

"Croak."

"Do I look stupid? Men don't suddenly turn into frogs. You're watching me, aren't you? And laughing at me for talking to a frog. Fred, come out at once!"

"Croak, croak."

Gemma stormed downstairs. The shopping list lay on the kitchen table where she had left it. She rushed to the window and expected to see an empty drive. Fred had gone out, she tried to convince herself, and somehow she had missed him. But the car was there next to Fred's bright green motorbike.

She folded her arms and stomped back to the foot of the stairs. "You won't catch me out," she shouted. "I'm not bothered. I'm going to play on-line bingo."

She didn't have time to log onto her favourite site as the frog hopped onto the keyboard. "Ugh!" she screamed and ran into the kitchen.

Later, when her nerves had settled, she crept back to the computer. The frog was still sitting there in front of a message on screen supposedly from

Fred. *Jumped onto bed and have been turned into frog.*

"Really?" Gemma sniggered. "And a wicked witch has cast a spell on you, what a shame."

The frog pressed a few keys and *dunno* appeared on the screen.

"Look, frogs in fairy tales can talk, why can't you?"

Can't...help me flashed up.

"How?" she shrugged.

The story, what happens?

"Simple, the princess kisses him and, bingo, he's back as the prince."

Kiss me then!

"I don't think so!"

Please...

Reluctantly Gemma touched the frog's slimy face with her finger and lowered her lips to meet his. "Yuk!" she cried jumping back.

Nothing happened.

Try again, please?

"This is gonna cost you Fred. This isn't a joke anymore, I've had enough."

Please, Gemma, please...I'll love you forever...promise.

Pressing her lips together, Gemma kissed the frog again. No result. Standing back, she said, "Perhaps I've got the story wrong? I'll google it."

Within seconds a version of the fairy tale was on screen. "Okay, the princess owes the frog a favour, so she offers him a home with her, never thinking he'd bother to move in. When he shows up, she gets angry, grabs him and throws him against a wall. He turns back into a prince and they live happily ever after."

Is that it?

"Yes."

Sounds painful. Can you try?

"No way! This really has gone far enough...and you're probably filming everything or worse...putting it all on the net. I can't harm a defenceless creature. It's wrong. This is another of your sad jokes Fred, isn't it? Frog, I don't know how you got in my house but you are so out of here!" Using both hands she scooped up the frog, carried him into the garden and deposited him on the lawn.

That night Gemma slept alone. Fred didn't show up. By next morning she was worried and talking to herself. "What can I do? People will think I'm crazy if I tell them my partner has turned into a frog and wants to be thrown against a wall."

The next couple of days she cleaned the house from roof space to ground level, mowed the lawn and weeded the flower borders. On the third night she went to a neighbour's barbeque.

"Fred's away," she said when people asked.

"Oh, never mind, come and meet my French cousin, Henri," said the hostess, "he's a chef."

"This chicken's delicious," said Gemma and picked up another bite-size piece from the platter Henri handed around.

"Not chicken," he insisted, "but the finest frogs' legs I've cooked in years. You English, why don't you eat them?"

"Maybe we don't know how to cook them," Gemma shrugged.

"Poaching is best. These frogs are from the garden. They're good because they're so fresh."

They were the first frogs' legs Gemma ate, but not the last. When she reported Fred missing at the police station, she didn't mention the frog incident. Occasionally, she wonders what really happened to him as she's not heard from him since. But she's not bothered because now she is living happily with Henri.

Under the Magnolia Tree
by John Carpenter

Jed had forgotten something important, but he knew he'd remember it if he could just lie under the Magnolia tree for a while. All he needed to do was stroll up the garden path.

That would have been easy if not for an inexplicably rapid nightfall that had left him in almost total darkness. There was a source of light behind him so he turned towards it, only to find more inexplicability.

The light was coming from a TV screen showing spectacular images of his garden. That was nonsensical. He didn't have CCTV and besides everything was pitch black. And how come the TV garden was so annoyingly superior to the real thing?

Take that perfectly-laid yellow-brick path. He hadn't even ordered the bricks yet. And that superb green arched gate. Oh yes, it was part of the grand design, but he'd found it so difficult to build that he'd cut corners.

Jed shrugged. "Either that's one hell of a garden makeover show or I've finally flipped!"

Light filtering through the gate onto the yellow bricks reminded him he'd been going somewhere, but the quality of the screen images distracted him. Was this some *Carlo Fandango* 3D effect? He recalled buying the TV, but not 3D. Those glasses and TV dinners didn't sit well together.

Perhaps he'd bought a more high-tech TV and forgotten. Now when did he last go to that electronics store? The question 'when' distracted him, first into wondering what time it was and then into acknowledging that his timeline had become a mash of disjointed memories. He didn't even know what year it was any more.

Maybe it was the Sixties and he'd popped Purple Haze or smoked too much Durban Poison and the always-surprising mind expansion phase was beginning. But if that were true, where did those vivid memories of a *Back to the Sixties* 60th birthday party come from? He could even recall a rumour about the fruit cup having a special ingredient.

The notion that he might be *fruit-cupped out* triggered the opening bars of *Voodoo Chile* in his mind's ear. His mind's eye joined it and presented him with Julia, dancing. Her beads swinging and her hands performing those beautiful Kathak moves she'd learned during their 'world tour' of India.

The Hendrix classic faded and mixed into the insistently sombre clanging of a church bell. His dancing wife cross-dissolved into a rainbow serpent slithering along a corridor of unprocessed emotion. He beheld a coffin and beside it a nurse - in tears! It was his daughter Karen and she was angry. Maybe with him? Had he done something wrong?

A rainbow-coloured head rose on a coiling body, exposing hypodermic fangs. Little shocks spiralled into a bigger shock. "My God! I've murdered my wife and I'm on Death Row."

A poisonous open mouth hurtled towards him.

"But wait a second!"

Overloaded fangs stopped mid-strike.

"That 'Being In Prison For Murder' thing is just a recurring nightmare. I always wake up a free man."

The serpent became the last glowing letter in a neon sign reading, 'hiss'.

Retreating to the safety of pseudo-psychology, Jed put it all down to his super-ego attacking his id.

The neon S crackled and shattered revealing the TV garden again, superficially innocuous, but more insidious on closer inspection.

Those ferns bordering the path, for instance, were made of intertwined rainbow-serpents trying to grab Jed's attention. The one swallowing its own tail and spinning like a Bhaktapur prayer wheel, succeeded. In half a split second, it had transported Jed back to his last LSD trip. Ornate mandalas encircled him and ancient voices, chanting primordial tones, suppressed his will to disengage. He was powerless and terrified, this time he might really die! Another rainbow serpent exposed its fangs.

Snap! Jed found himself on the yellow-brick path inside the TV garden.

Sherlock Homes, having just clicked his forefinger and thumb together, smiled thinly.

"Apologies, I had no wish to startle you, only to help you focus." Jed remained startled. Holmes pressed on, "We have not a moment to waste. So forgive me for being so direct, but may I ask if you have remembered yet?"

"How did you know I'd forgotten something?"

"Elementary my dear Jed, I can also assure you that the limited time you have to remember grows steadily more limited. Observe the gate."

Following Holmes' pointing finger, Jed noticed that the gate seemed less open than before. "So what," thought Jed, "and how come he knows my name?" The fictional detective's deductive powers were impressive on the TV screen, but from inside the TV garden Jed found being on the receiving end a lot less comfortable. So he was relieved when another familiar figure arrived.

"Lieutenant Colombo, The Angels Police Department. I apologise, sir, but Holmes is exceptionally gifted if a little short on people skills."

"Did you say *The Angels Police Department?*" The phrase spooked Jed.

Colombo, thumb to forehead, smiled. "Well, sir, it's my wife. She prefers English to Spanish. I told her *Los Angeles* is English these days, but you know how women are. Sometimes it's easier to just agree and the thing is, sir, my wife, like most women, is a better detective than I'll ever be when it comes to feelings."

The words 'wife' and 'feelings', seemed like clues to what Jed needed to remember. The yellow-brick path, less illuminated than before by the steadily-closing gate, was the final clue leading to a light-bulb moment. It was Julia's grand design that had somehow been implemented in this TV garden. But the real gate wasn't built to her plan and her yellow-brick path hadn't even been started. In reality, he'd let Julia down, hadn't he?

The hissing of the rainbow serpents grew venomously louder. Colombo moved closer.

Holmes produced a light sabre and took a step into the ferns. "Please be terse, lieutenant. Severed rainbow-serpent heads are generally replaced by two new ones."

Colombo nodded and continued. "Now sir, I'm sure you've heard of Peter Falk the actor who played the fictional character Lieutenant Colombo."

The light sabre flashed and rainbow-coloured heads flew in all directions creating unique psychedelic effects. "Lieutenant, I really must insist you come to the point."

Colombo shrugged resignedly. "I'm sorry sir, but Holmes is right. There's not much time. So the fact is sir, Peter Falk...well to be blunt sir, he's dead." There was a pause while Colombo inspected Jed's blank face.

Holmes, spattered with rainbow coloured blood, chimed in, "Alas, Jed, nobody lives forever. Not even me and certainly not the actor who portrayed your favourite version of me. Jeremy Brett, sadly, is long gone."

There followed another unnatural pause while Colombo scrutinised Jed's unresponsive face and sighed, "Well sir, it pains me to say this, but we need to go to Plan B."

"Plan B? I didn't even know there was a Plan A!" cried Jed.

"About time, if I may make so bold," shouted Holmes, slicing through both heads of a two-headed serpent.

"Lookout Holmes!" cried Colombo pointing to a huge bat swooping quickly down from behind.

Holmes produced a wooden tennis racket, and skilfully backhand smashed the leather-winged aggressor into the ferns where it was devoured by rainbow serpents. "Game, set but not, I fancy, match, lieutenant. Other mega-chiroptera will follow, undoubtedly providing stiffer opposition." He forced a brief smile before re-engaging with the temporarily distracted rainbow serpents. "Could we perhaps expedite matters lieutenant?"

Colombo patted himself down and located his notebook. "Nothing to worry about, sir, just routine." He flipped some pages and tapped one with his forefinger. "Head office asked me to make a note sir. It's your wife...I'm afraid she's made a formal complaint."

"Oh no! I'll bet it's about the garden isn't it?"

"Well sir, if you'd just like to step through that gate. As quickly as you can, sir."

As Jed looked at the last slivers of light on the yellow-brick path, it finally dawned on him that he really didn't have much time. He made a mad dash, but it was too little too late.

Struggling to squeeze through the narrowing gap, he saw the Magnolia tree and remembered where he'd been going. The blossoms were giving out so much light that he could only just make out the exceptionally familiar figure on the grass beneath.

It was Julia, but she was lying very still. My God, if she were dead, he'd never be able to apologise to her about the garden!

Jed fought harder, but the gate only squeezed him tighter so that he could hardly breathe. Behind him, Holmes and Colombo stopped pushing.

"It's no use Holmes, we're just helping to suffocate him."

"Yes, lieutenant, you're right, but there may be another way. Would you be so kind as to hand me that remote control?"

Jed, struggling to breathe, gasped, "Julia, I'm sorry..." and passed out.

****

He wasn't aware of Holmes scanning endless TV archives and finally exclaiming, "Eureka!" He didn't hear the Lone Ranger gallop up the yellow-brick path or feel the impact of Silver's hooves on the green arched gate forcing it open just enough to allow Colombo and Holmes to push him through.

Jed only heard a fading cry of "Hi Ho Silver Away" as he landed on the grass next to Julia. Though she looked exactly as she'd looked the day they'd met, she wasn't breathing.

"Oh God! I'm too late." Jed started sobbing like a frightened infant.

Julia took a dramatic in-breath and opened her eyes alarmingly wide.

"Julia, you're alive!" He was so shocked, he stopped crying.

"Alive!" she laughed scornfully. "I might have been, but for you."

"Me! What did I do?"

"Who took me out for candle-lit dinners, fed me chocolate and forced champagne down my neck?" Jed was speechless. "All that high romance shortened my life by a good two weeks."

"Oh so that's what you complained about."

Julia looked upwards and shook her head.

Jed, in a pathetic attempt to placate her, blurted out, "I'm sorry...and I'm sorry about the garden too."

Julia gave an exasperated snort and lay back on the grass. Jed knew enough to say no more and for some moments they both gazed through the white blossoms as they had done many times over the years.

After a while she said, "They told me I could help by making a complaint."

"'They?"

"The angels."

"Oh now I get it! The Angels Police Department."

"I don't know what you're on about Jed, but it's high time to stop talking...and thinking for that matter. You need to feel your way. You do remember how to do that, don't you?"

She offered him her most tender smile. "It's time to go home, now."

Jed's bottom lip trembled. "Do you really have to go Julia?"

She sighed. "Don't be such a baby, Jed, I'm already gone and you know it. Now it's time for you to let go of me. Time to find a real feeling – one that you can keep for good."

Jed opened his eyes. He was under the Magnolia tree and the sun was high in the sky. He thought it must be mid-afternoon.

A carrier bag lay next to him and he could just see the top of a small urn through its white plastic folds. He took the tiny vessel out, removed the lid and let it roll across his fingers onto the grass. As he watched Julia's ashes escape into the warm air, he felt completely at peace with himself again.

Jed closed his eyes and discovered he could look through the sky and the stars into distant galaxies. Most importantly, he discovered in himself a feeling of immense gratitude for the unique gift that had been his life. The feeling came to him like his oldest, truest friend; the one who had never abandoned him, not even in his darkest hour.

Quite alone, but feeling far from lonely, Jed entered the palace of the Great Bear and danced his last waltz to the rhythm of his dying breaths. Coming and going and coming and going and finally, gone.

****

Karen had been called by the school to say that her father hadn't arrived to walk his grand-children home. She'd phoned her husband and had driven straight to her parent's house. She found him under the Magnolia tree and it was obvious straight-away that he was dead. Even so she followed her medical training to confirm what she already knew.

Kneeling next to him, she picked up the carrier bag and looked inside; two DVD box sets - *Sherlock Holmes The Complete Collection* and *Colombo Seasons 1-7;* a VHS video - *The Lone Ranger's Triumph;* and a photo of her mother at a recent *Back to the Sixties* 60th birthday party. So those were the things her father had 'needed' to collect on his way to the school.

A telly addict to the end and one with such a contented death mask that she didn't want to cry. Instead she lay down next to him, like she'd done as a child, and stared up through the blossoms until she'd completely lost track of time.

Five or ten or maybe even twenty minutes later, Karen pressed *Him Indoors* on her mobile. Her husband answered immediately. "Karen?"

"It's Dad. I think his heart must have given out."

"Oh my God! Are you OK, love?"

"Just get here as soon as you can."

She touched the red button without waiting for him to answer and stared up at the sky again. It had been only two weeks since her dad had found her mother's body under the Magnolia tree. They were still waiting for the results of that inquest. Now they would have to wait for another one. She recalled one of her dad's remarks on the subject of inquests and funerals. "Only for the living. Makes no difference at all to the dead person."

Karen still had a few minutes before her husband arrived and the whole traumatic emotional pantomime began again. A few minutes in which she could let go and feel a very real and uniquely beautiful feeling that she been introduced to by her parents through cloud-gazing under the Magnolia tree

A feeling that is available to everyone from the first in-breath to the last out-breath - the feeling of gratitude for simply being alive.

The River Crossing by Brian Johnson

I am wheeled into the intensive care unit in the middle of the night. They make me comfortable and elevate my bed slightly. I am left to survey my immediate surroundings.

Five beds opposite mine, but where there should have been a bed, a gap where a nurse has placed a chair. When I look again, strangely there's a lady sitting there, but I don't take much notice of her – and yet, did she smile at me?

The nursing staff are busy and the central lights are fully on glaring down on us. The corner bed has the curtains drawn with at least two nurses working there. In the other corner a figure sleeps.

I am sure that lady is smiling at me again. Very strange, as no one is allowed visitors for 24 hours. I look again at the lady and yes, she did smile at me.

The person in the bed to my right must have

seen me staring at the lady. "'Ello mate," he said.

Mate? I don't like that.

"Dennis, that's me, what you in for, mate?"

I want to say, "I'm not your bloody mate," but I hold back. The lady sitting on the chair, she smiles at me again. She is wearing a couple of thin scarves or shawls made of very soft lightweight material, red, like her hair. Oh yes, her hair, red, or is it?

"Laddie in the corner, he won't make it, mate, can't see him pulling through. Motor bike crash."

I turn my head. I can't move my torso. Wires. Drains. I am so sore.

The bed to my left is taken by a female patient, she's sleeping. I wish I could.

My God, the lady from the chair is near to me. I hadn't been aware of her moving. Yet, here she is at my bedside, smiling at me.

Oddly, I thought she was a redhead, red like the scarves draped around her shoulders, but close up I see she is a blonde. The nurses aren't bothered by my visitor. I wonder why? There's a pungent scent in the air. What is it? Ah, yes, of course it's honeysuckle. I have honeysuckle growing up my patio at home.

"Would you like to come with me now Brian?" she asks.

That a vision of loveliness like her is speaking to me makes me feel utterly at ease. She leans towards me and I see her scarves are fastened with a clip in the form of two interlocking birds. And her perfume is honeysuckle, lovely.

A nurse comes to look at Dennis but takes no notice of my visitor.

My lady visitor leans over me. "Are you

feeling more rested, sweetheart?" she asks in a soft voice. She adjusts her cloak and pulls the hood up over her hair. Strange, I wasn't aware she had been wearing a cloak before. And her hair is blonde. Yes, her blonde hair is fastened in a pony tail falling forward over her shoulder.

I feel so at ease that my words are uttered before I can constrain myself, "Am I dying? If so, I never realised death could be so beautiful. Where is the figure with the scythe?"

My lady smiles an understanding smile. "If you mean the Grim Reaper, we mainly call on him for major catastrophes like earthquakes, famine, war and so on." She touches my arm. "Come along now, we must not be late," she pauses, "we have a schedule to keep."

Within minutes we are joining many others, quite a procession heading down a walkway to the banks of a river. What had previously been sunny weather changed to a rapidly developing dense fog.

"Oh, dear," said my lady, "we have missed the boatman."

I glimpse the outline of a figure in a boat using a long stern pole as the mist swirls around him. Only the glimmer of his mast lantern remains until it, too, is engulfed in the thickening mist.

My lady sighs. "I must leave you here. But don't worry, if you make your way up to the waiting cafeteria, someone will look after you."

As I climb up the river bank I pass a large wooden sign, 'Styx River Crossing'.

Someone is speaking to me. There's a slight pressure on my face. Opening my eyes, a staff nurse beams at me.

"That's it Brian, come back to me. It's time for your pills and I need to change your dressing. It's going to sting a bit, but only for a minute."

She leans across me and the fabric of her uniform stretches. Her ponytail drops onto her shoulder. Blonde, yes blonde.

The scent of her perfume lingers and my eyes are drawn to her trim waist. It's encircled with a belt, held in place with a buckle in the shape of a bird.

"That's it sweetheart," she says and smiles at me. "You are going to be fine, just fine, very soon, matey!"

In the corner, the motorbike lad is heavily bandaged and plastered. One of his arms is encased in a cage and supported with a bracket attached to his waist. As he waves his free arm weakly, I readily return his gesture of greeting.

Opposite me a bed has been moved into the once empty space. The occupant in the other corner appears to be sleeping, as is the lady to my left.

The bed to my right is empty, newly re-made, pristine and ready.

Matey? She called me matey. How very, very nice.

Cigarettes Are Bad For Your Health
By Carol Bennion-Pedley

It's a vicious circle. I smoke because of my stressful life as a single mother but, thinking about that Christmas week, my life would have been so much less stressful if I just hadn't stopped for that packet of cigarettes.

I had to work full time, so therefore my youngest son, age five at that time, had no choice but to go to the 'out-of-school' club. I was on my way to collect him when I thought I would spare the two minutes it took to stop off at my local supermarket to buy fresh vegetables for the evening meal. Okay, I lie, I needed cigarettes, desperately.

The car park was packed this close to Christmas but I happily parked at the top end and ran inside. I had just purchased my much-needed cigarettes when all hell broke loose. Alarms started going off, staff ran to the doors and refused to let anyone leave. An announcement was made over the tannoy – 'code black, code black', to which two dozen members of staff responded by running to the front of the store and through the doors. There were a couple of the butchers in there and, I must admit, I looked down for meat cleavers in their hands but, to my disappointment, couldn't see any. The doors were closed and locked behind them. We, the valuable customers, were safe, for now.

No-one knew what was going on so, being British, we started rumours. By the time the Chinese whispers had reached the back of the store, the car park was being taken over by gun-wielding robbers, dozens of them, all coming for us. Someone had already been shot and died.

Through the doors, we saw the ambulance and four police cars draw up outside, numerous policemen and women jumping out and running toward something. I couldn't see any guns, so I assumed the rumours were wrong. And how wrong they were!

The true story was this: two elderly ladies, who really should have known better, both decided they wanted the one available car park space, both felt they were each entitled to it and, like something out of a cartoon, it ended in a fight between them. Well done to our local supermarket though for their quick reactions, very impressive.

All of which made me late to pick up my son, which meant I had missed speaking to his teacher. I assume she had tried to stay around to see me, got fed up with waiting and left a message with my son instead.

And so the message I got was, "My teacher says it's our nativity play tomorrow so can we please have my costume, I'm playing the son."

I looked down at him, and, very gently, asked, "Have you been given any letters to give to me recently?"

"Yes, but I put them down in the out-of-school club and lost them," he replied innocently.

Well, how could I possibly be mad? My son had the lead role; after all, he was the Son of God, Jesus himself. I spent all evening sewing various tea towels and sheets together, making a costume worthy of such a part. Right up until bedtime when my darling son asked me when I was going to make his costume.

"What do you think we've been doing all evening?" I asked. Which is when he informed me, he was not the son, he was the Sun, you know, that shines brightly in the sky.

He went to bed; and I went outside for the first of many cigarettes that night.

I awoke the next morning with a start, mainly because of the bright yellow paint glaring at me. I sat up. Just great. I had fallen asleep on the large circle of cardboard I had cut out from a box I'd found and then covered with the left over paint from the lemon walls in the hallway.

The teacher looked at me as I dropped off my son and his costume at school. I smiled at her. I think she recognised a sleep-deprived parent enough to ignore the yellow streak running through my hair.

Of course, I attended the nativity play. One of the wise men wet himself but the tea towel on his head came in handy so that was okay.

My own child shone brightly. I waved to him. He waved back, and then frowned at the little girl standing next to him who burst into tears.

I needed a coffee...and a cigarette!

About the Contributors

Carol Bennion-Pedley is a woman of a 'certain' age, with the hot flushes and irritability that comes with it and is extremely self-opinionated. But she also comes with four amazing grown up children and one perfect grandson, all of whom give her inspiration for short stories and blogging - so she must have done something right!

John Carpenter has a career as Technical Author that spans more than thirty years and includes working on Michael Crichton's book *La Vita Elettronica* published by Garzanti in 1983. In addition to the UK, he has lived and worked in Italy, France and the Netherlands and in 2003 appeared in a short film shot in Spain. He has written several TV and film scripts that are registered with Writer's Guild of America and has been a resident of Burton upon Trent since 1999. He joined the writing group this year and has just begun studying a part-time degree course in animation at the University of Derby.

Josie Elson is a mother and grandmother, and is now retired. A founder member of Burton Monday Writers, she prefers writing children's stories, but will have a go at anything!

Mary Gladstone is a widow with four adult children. She has had a variety of occupations, including running a B&B. She was a foster mother for many years. Her hobbies are reading, music, writing, history and her grandchildren.

Brian Johnson (or BJ) has been involved with writing for over forty years. He finds it not only relaxing but also, as is generally accepted, very therapeutic. Writing serves as a natural channel to occupy long winter nights as television can be addictively soul destroying.

Ann Hodgkin is a long standing member of the group. She has had a variety of work published and has been successful in numerous competitions. Her favourite genre however, is the short story.

Maggs Payne enjoys writing in any genre, but has been most successful with her poetry. Maggs is proud to be part of such a successful group that continues to go from strength to strength. She is founder member and also Honorary President.

Maria Soldano was born in Argentina where she studied drawing, painting and sculpture. Her work has been exhibited in South America and Europe. She currently lives and works in Spain and her paintings can be seen on www.artelista.com

Barbara Swallow has been a member of Burton Monday Writers for twelve years. She enjoys writing short stories and the company of other writers.

Lynda Turner has had three historical romantic novels published under her pen name **Lynda Dunwell**. Her first novel was a contender for the RNA Joan Hessayon award in 2012 and her second novel short listed at the UK Festival of Romance 2012 in the short romance category. She is also a prize-winning short story writer and has sold several stories to the women's magazine market. Excerpts of her work are on her website at www.lyndadunwell.com.

Shelagh Wain is a retired teacher and crossword addict, who enjoys writing in any genre, but prefers monologues and poetry.

FLIGHTS OF FANCY

Made in the USA
Charleston, SC
22 November 2013